I0590357

The Unanticipated Storm
© 2025 Danielle Amour. All rights reserved.
ISBN: 979-8-9942047-0-2

This is a work of fiction. Names, characters, businesses, places, events, and incidents are either the products of the author's imagination or used in a fictitious manner. Any resemblance to actual persons, living or dead, or actual events is purely coincidental.

Content Warning:

This novel contains themes and scenes that may be difficult for some readers.
It includes references to sexual assault, emotional trauma, grief, depression, and anxiety.
While these elements are portrayed with sensitivity and purpose, readers are encouraged to care for their well-being and pause as needed. If you have experienced trauma or loss, please prioritize self-care while reading.
Resources and support are available through the National Sexual Assault Hotline **(1-800-656-4673)** and the **988 Suicide & Crisis Lifeline.**

Dedication

For my son —

Knowing I have someone looking up to me and depending on me gave me the strength to find my way back to writing. You reminded me of who I am, and who I'm still becoming. Every word of this book exists because you inspired me to keep going. I thank God for blessing me with you every day and I love you more than words can describe.

Author's Note

There are moments in life when everything we thought we understood about love, trust, and healing gets tested by something we never saw coming. *The Unanticipated Storm* was born from that space — the fragile, beautiful in-between where pain meets growth.

Jaida and Jackson's story isn't just about romance; it's about rediscovering yourself after life breaks you open. It's about learning that healing doesn't always look graceful, and that love—real love—sometimes shows up when we've stopped looking for it.

If you've ever weathered a storm that changed you, this story is for you. I hope it reminds you that even in your quietest moments of uncertainty, you're never beyond repair. Sometimes, the storm isn't meant to destroy you, it's meant to reveal who you were always meant to be.

With love,

Danielle Amour

Chapter One

Under Pressure

The morning started like any other workday morning—or at least it tried to. Sunlight peeked through the curtains in thin, golden lines, warming the lavender-scented air lingering from the diffuser on Jaida's dresser. The room felt peaceful, but Jaida did not.

Sleep had eluded her the night before—her mind restless, thoughts racing through her head like a storm she couldn't calm. When sleep finally came, it arrived in short, broken increments, never more than two hours at a time. By the time her alarm sounded that morning, dragging herself out of bed felt like lifting a thousand-pound weight.

The repetitive chime went off again, and again, until she pushed herself upright, untangling the rumpled sheets twisted around her legs. She had hit snooze as many times as she could get away with before finally forcing her feet to the floor.

From the kitchen came the familiar whirl of the blender— pineapple, ginger, kale, and a scoop of unflavored collagen protein powder she blended into her morning smoothie. It was routine, something she could hold onto when everything else felt unsteady.

After her shower, Jaida misted the air lightly with Jo Malone's Peony & Blush Suede before dabbing the cologne onto her wrists and collarbone. Her hair was pulled back into a simple ponytail. She slipped into her turquoise scrubs and stepped into her Avia, smart and comfortable, tennis shoes.

Minimal makeup—just chapstick and sheer gloss. Nothing more. Nothing extra. Just enough to enhance her natural beauty and make her feel like herself.

She caught her reflection in the mirror and forced a quiet breath. Confident, she reminded herself. Capable. Even if she didn't feel it this morning, she had earned her place. She had her dream job—one people hoped for, applied for, waited years to get into. Openings in her department were scarce, and management picked only the best. And they picked her.

Outside, the dew on the blades of green grass shimmered in the fresh, crisp air, a sharp contrast to the heaviness sitting in her chest.

Despite everything, she made it to work on time.

The moment she stepped onto the surgical prep and recovery unit, the familiar chaos wrapped around her like a weighted blanket she didn't know she needed. The smell of freshly brewed coffee drifted from the nurses' station— strong, slightly burnt, and already on its second pot of the morning.

Harsh fluorescent lighting buzzed overhead, washing the hallways in that sterile, unmistakable hospital glow. Call lights blinked on the unit board like restless fireflies, each one demanding attention. A telemetry alarm buzzed from a nearby room—persistent, shrill, impossible to ignore. Voices drifted from the hallway: night shift giving report, family members asking questions, nurses coordinating care.

A phlebotomist's cart squeaked down the linoleum floor, wheels wobbling under the weight of tubes and labeled specimen bags. And beneath it all, the steady chorus of IV pumps beeped in rhythmic protest.

Normally, the sensory overload made her tense. But today? Today, it was a distraction that grounded her. Kept her from drifting into the thoughts she was avoiding. Staying busy meant she didn't have to sit with the storm inside her.

As hoped, the day hit the ground running. By 7:30 AM, Jaida was fully immersed in the whirlwind of patient care—vitals, assessments, chart checks, pain meds, surgical dressings, patient questions, surgeon rounds. The floor was a carousel that never stopped spinning.

When she finally sat down at 10:30 AM, it was the first pause she'd had all morning. She sank into the stiff break-room chair with a sigh. She only had 30 minutes to chart, pee, and grab a quick snack before beginning afternoon medication rounds at 11:00 AM. She calculated the timing in her head like a math equation she'd solved a thousand times.

By 12:15 PM, she was wrapping up the medication pass—an act that felt like a small victory on such a hectic unit. Falling behind on passing meds meant an uphill battle the rest of the day, one she didn't have the energy to fight.

She sat and rushed to finish charting on her fourth patient when the charge nurse paged her overhead.

New post-op admission.

Of course.

Not her favorite assignment. She preferred pre-ops—the patients who walked in alert, oriented, still whole. Post-ops were different. They arrived groggy, vulnerable, sometimes in pain, sometimes scared. And today, that luck simply wasn't on her side.

Jaida took a breath and squared her shoulders. The day wasn't slowing down for her. And she wasn't expecting it to.

Before her new patient arrived on the unit, Jaida finished charting on her fourth patient and began to skim the incoming patient's chart. 47-year-old female that was being admitted under surgical observation after Hemorrhoid surgery. Local anesthesia, no drains, minimal fluid loss.

Straightforward on paper, but she knew better—pain could hit hard, mobility could be difficult, and patients often arrived frustrated, embarrassed, or miserable. She read quickly through the notes, memorizing the surgeon's orders, pain plan, and allergies.

Once she had a general picture, the weight of the nonstop morning caught up to her all at once. Her stomach tightened with hunger she'd ignored too long. She needed a quick lunch before she met the new arrival.

Jaida slipped into the break room, nudging the door open with her hip. The air inside felt slightly warmer, stale in a way only hospital break rooms could manage. A faint haze lingered near the ceiling, and the unmistakable smell of burnt popcorn hit her immediately, sharp, charred, and clinging stubbornly to the walls. Someone must have scorched a bag earlier and then fled the scene.

The small room held the same tired setup it always had: one round table in the center surrounded by mismatched plastic chairs, a microwave with fingerprints smudged across the handle, and a refrigerator plastered with outdated potluck flyers and a "CLEAN OUT BY FRIDAY" sign no one ever obeyed. Along the back wall stood a row of grey metal lockers, the kind that rattled whenever the HVAC kicked on.

An empty coffee pot sat on the warmer, the glass bottom browned and crusted from sitting too long on heat. The smell of bitter, burned residue floated up, mixing with the popcorn disaster hanging in the air.

Another nurse from the unit sat slouched at the table, eating from a small plastic container. She barely glanced up when Jaida walked in, offering only a tired half-nod—the silent greeting of nurses who had already used up every word they had for the day.

Jaida opened her bag, pulled out her sandwich with thin sliced honey roasted turkey, and leaned against the counter. The hum of the refrigerator and the buzz of the fluorescent light above filled the quiet space. For a moment, the break room felt like a small island—unpretty, unglamorous, but sheltered from the alarms and demands waiting on the other side of the door.

She took a breath, bracing herself. Her new patient was on the way, and the day wasn't slowing down for anyone.

With her sandwich in one hand, she reached the other hand to the cool doorknob, about to exit the breakroom and return to the unit, when her phone buzzed. She turned around, sat down at the table and checked the message.

> **Jackson:** Good Afternoon. I hope you are having a great day.

Usually, a text from Jackson brought a smile to her face, especially on days like this. But today, it hit differently. It was a reminder of the very reality she was working so hard to avoid.

I guess I can't run and hide, she thought as she typed her response.

> **Jaida:** Good Afternoon. Thank you. It is going okay, just busy.

> **Jackson:** I am sure it is not anything you cannot handle. What time do you get off?

> **Jaida:** Thanks, 4pm.

> **Jackson:** Just a few more hours, Boo. Then you can go home and relax.

Jaida: Not today. I'm going to the Emergency Department when I get off.

Jackson: What time are you going there?

Jaida: As soon as I get off.

Jackson: Oh okay. I'm sure everything will be okay. Keep me posted.

Before she could reply, her work phone rang. It was the Post Anesthesia Care Unit (PACU) calling with report.

"Surgical unit, Jaida speaking," she answered.

"Hi, this is Hope down in PACU calling to give report on Ms. Peacock."

"Hey Hope, it's Jaida the float nurse. How are you?" Jaida recognized her voice instantly. Hope was one of the few people who always sounded cheerful, even over the phone.

They exchanged pleasantries and Hope reminded Jaida she was welcome to shadow in PACU anytime—pending manager approval, of course. Jaida responded with her usual diplomatic optimism, even though inside, she felt like a wreck. She couldn't let it show.

Fifteen minutes later, Ms. Peacock arrived on the floor, matching Hope's report perfectly—a rare relief.

Ms. Peacock looked around the assigned room as the transportation escort rolled her stretcher down the hallway and parked it just outside the door. Her new room was single-private, unshared, and blessedly quiet compared to the hustle of the recovery area. Jaida met them in the hall with a warm, professional smile.

"My name is Jaida, and I'll be your nurse," she said, stepping closer.

Ms. Peacock returned the smile, her expression softening with relief.

The escort pushed the stretcher into the room and positioned it alongside the bed. As he locked the wheels, Ms. Peacock's eyes traveled slowly across the space. A television was mounted neatly on the wall across from the bed. Crisp white linens were tucked tight, the kind that made straight lines look effortless. An IV pole stood waiting beside the bed, metal shining under the overhead lights.

"Alright, Ms. Peacock," Jaida said gently, moving to the bedside. "I'm going to help you transfer over to the bed. I'll walk you through it."

With calm, clear instructions, Jaida guided her through the shift—small scoots, a careful turn, a controlled slide. Ms. Peacock followed each step, wincing slightly but determined. Within moments, she was settled onto the fresh bed, the stretcher pulled away and rolled out of the room.

"Perfect," Jaida said, raising the head of the bed a little. "Let's get you comfortable." She reached for the vitals machine clipped to the stand above the nightstand and pressed the power button. The screen flickered to life with a soft beep. One by one, she placed the blood pressure cuff around Ms. Peacock's arm, clipped the pulse ox to her finger, positioned the thermometer, and glanced at the clock as she began to record her respirations.

As the machine hummed and cycled, Jaida asked, "How's your pain right now?"

Ms. Peacock hesitated, then gave a number. Jaida nodded, making mental notes as she lifted the gown slightly to do a quick skin assessment—checking color, incisions, pressure points, and any signs of discomfort.

When she finished, she stepped back and reached for the paper menu sitting on the counter. "If you'd like a drink or a snack before lunch gets here, I can grab something from the patient food area. Water, juice, crackers—just let me know what sounds good."

Ms. Peacock accepted the menu, her fingers brushing the edges as she looked it over, finally exhaling in the calm of her new room.

Jaida handed Ms. Peacock the call light, placing it gently in her palm. "This is your call light," she said, making sure the cord wasn't tangled. "If you need anything at all—pain medicine, help getting up, or just someone to check in—press this red button. I'll be right back."

Ms. Peacock nodded, her expression easing now that the worst part of the transition was behind her.

With one last glance to ensure her patient was comfortable, pillows fluffed and vitals cycling smoothly, Jaida stepped out of the room. The hallway greeted her with its familiar soundtrack—IV pumps chiming, a call light pinging from down the hall, someone laughing near the nurses' station, a workstation computer on wheels squeaking as it rolled over uneven tiles.

She inhaled slowly, centering herself. Four more patients to check on before she could finally sit down and chart the admission. She tucked the clipboard under her arm and headed down the hall, her steps quick but steady, her mind already sorting through the next dozen tasks waiting for her.

Then it struck her—she hadn't used the bathroom all day. Not once. The nonstop rush had swallowed every basic need. With a quiet sigh, she ducked into the nearest restroom to finally take a moment for herself.

By 3:35 PM, she handed off report to the oncoming nurse and practically bolted out of the unit. No matter how much she loved nursing, the end of her shift always washed over her like a release—gratitude, relief, and the deep exhale that came with finally being done.

The transition from the hospital to the outside world was always strange, almost jarring. One moment she was in the bright, humming chaos of the unit—call lights blinking, alarms beeping, voices overlapping. The next, she was stepping into the dimmer, quieter hospital corridor that led toward the elevators. Each step away from the unit lightened her shoulders, like layers of invisible weight slipping off.

She pushed through the employee entrance and out into the late afternoon air. The automatic doors whooshed shut behind her, cutting off the sterile brightness of the hospital and replacing it with the warm scent of pavement and the fading notes of sunlight stretching across the parking garage. The world looked different out here—less harsh, less demanding.

She made her way across the garage, her pace fast but her posture softening with each step. Her ponytail swayed against the back of her scrubs. Her shoulders rolled out, no longer tensed for the next alarm or urgent call. She unlocked her car, slid inside, and let herself sink into the seat, lips parting to release a breath she didn't even realize she'd been holding.

She pulled out of the garage and headed toward home on autopilot—muscle memory guiding her through familiar turns and exits. But with every passing block, the pit in her stomach grew heavier, darker, reminding her of the detour she needed to make. The Emergency Department.

Her body reacted before the thought fully settled—her grip tightened around the steering wheel, her shoulders curled slightly inward, and her foot eased off the accelerator. Her breathing shifted to shallow, measured pulls of air. She blinked twice, anchoring herself.

Then she reached for her phone, tapped Pandora, and selected her favorite station—90s R&B.

As the opening notes of SWV's "Weak" flowed through the car, something in her unclenched. The harmonies, the soft synth, the familiar rhythm—music from that era always held a way of wrapping her up, soothing the parts of her she didn't show anyone. Today, she needed that anchor more than she wanted to admit.

When the song ended, the last note fading into silence, she sat still for a moment with both hands resting on the steering wheel. She closed her eyes, inhaled deeply through her nose, and whispered to herself, barely audible: "You got this, Jai. You can do this."

Then she exhaled, opened her eyes, and stepped out of the car.

Chapter Two

Beneath the Surface

The automatic doors of the hospital's Emergency Department slid open, revealing something Jaida wasn't expecting—a metal detector positioned front and center. That was new.

She paused for half a second, then stepped forward. The security officer motioned kindly, but firmly, while saying "Bag check, please."

She handed it over, lifted her arms slightly as instructed, and waited for the scan. The scent of disinfectant and floor polish from the ED lobby drifted toward her, sharp and unmistakable. When her bag was returned, she gave the officer a polite nod and forced a small smile before stepping fully inside.

The Emergency Department felt like walking into a blank page. White—everywhere. White furniture lined the walls, white chairs filled with patients and families, white floors so polished they reflected the overhead lights. The walls were plain white too, interrupted only by signage pointing toward triage, registration, and restrooms. And the nurses—every one of them—moved through the unit in crisp white scrubs, looking almost ghostlike against the sterile backdrop. The coldness of the space seeped into her skin.

A line formed at the check-in window, and Jaida joined it. Her breath hitched as she looked around. A man coughing into his elbow. Someone pacing. Someone praying quietly. The distant chirp of a cardiac monitor. A triage nurse calling a name.

Then the fear hit. Her heart pounded—heavy, fast, a drum against her ribs. She tried the deep breathing she taught her own patients: in through the nose, out through the mouth. But the air stuck in her chest. Her lungs felt too tight to expand fully. She looked calm on the outside—years of nursing had trained her for that—but internally, she was spiraling.

Her palms grew damp. Her knees felt loose. A warmth crawled up her neck. No. Not here. Not in front of all these people. She needed a plan.

Quietly, she pulled her phone from her scrub pocket and opened her Notes app. Her thumbs hesitated for a moment, trembling just slightly, then she began typing out the reason for her visit—the thing she couldn't bring herself to say aloud in this crowded waiting room, not with strangers three feet away on all sides. She typed the words she couldn't trust her voice to carry. And as she typed, she hoped—prayed—that this wouldn't be the moment her world tipped over completely.

When she reached the front of the line, she handed over her ID and insurance card to the woman behind the glass window, who wore a badge that read *Monica Mills*. Monica typed steadily, eyes flicking between her computer screen and the documents.

As Jaida waited, she glanced around again—nurses passing by, patients shifting in chairs, staff walking in and out of triage. Too many ears. Too little privacy.

Then Monica asked, "And what brings you in today?" Jaida hesitated. Her throat closed around the answer. She turned her phone toward Monica.

Monica's eyes moved over the note, slow and steady, her expression unchanged—no raised brows, no tightening around her mouth. Just a calm, practiced steadiness shaped by years of watching people walk in carrying fear heavier than their bags.

The hum of the printers and the soft shuffle of the waiting room filled the space between them as she absorbed Jaida's words. No judgment. Only a quiet, almost imperceptible empathy softening her gaze.

"All right," she said gently, sliding open a drawer. The patient's ID bracelet clicked against her nails as she lifted it, the plastic still warm from her touch.

She reached through the window for Jaida's wrist. Her hands were cool, steady, careful—never fumbling, never rushed. With a soft snap, the bracelet closed around Jaida's skin.

"You're all set. Have a seat, and someone will call you shortly." Monica offered a small, reassuring nod before instructing her back toward the waiting room with a subtle gesture, the kind that said *you're safe here* without a single word spoken.

"Thank you," Jaida said softly.

"You're welcome," Monica replied, giving her a small, understanding smile.

Then, Jaida walked to an empty seat in the waiting area, and whatever steadiness that smile offered dissolved almost instantly.

The space felt claustrophobic, heavy with agitation and illness. Harsh fluorescent lights bleached the room in an unforgiving glow. A man coughed openly near the corner, no mask, each wet hack cutting through the air like a warning. The scent of antiseptic clashed with the faint, stale smell of fast food wrappers. Every sensory detail pressed into her, tightening the coil of anxiety already wound in her chest.

Her phone vibrated and she looked down at the glowing screen to see Jackson's name flashing with a new message. She didn't want to open it—not yet. The disappointment hit first, heavy and familiar. She was here, scared and alone, and the man who'd pushed her into this situation wasn't beside her.

He should be here with me since he is the reason I had to come here in the first place, she thought, jaw tightening as she slid her thumb across the screen.

She finally opened the message.

Jackson: Hey Boo, you make it yet?

Jaida: Yes I am here. Still waiting.

Jackson: How long have you been there?

Jaida: Over an hour. Feels like forever. I'm nervous.

Jackson: Understandable. But you'll be fine.

Jaida: I hope you're right.

Jackson: Everything will be okay.

She read his last message twice, then let the phone fall gently into her lap. His words were meant to soothe, she knew that—but they landed like a hollow echo. A promise without presence. A reassurance she couldn't quite feel.

Around her, the waiting room buzzed on, loud and indifferent. And Jaida sat there, trying to hold herself together in a place that made her feel as small and exposed as she'd ever felt.

Jaida had almost grown accustomed to the constant motion of the Emergency Department—the automatic doors sliding open, the triage nurse calling patient names, the shuffle of people moving in every direction— she hadn't realized how easily she could tune out everything else. That is, until she heard it: her name.

"Jaida Evans," a clear, steady voice called from the triage area.

Startled, she looked up, heart skipping a beat, and rose from the waiting room chair.

"Right this way," the nurse said, extending an arm and guiding her back toward the triage rooms. Her skin the tone of Werther's caramel hard candy. She wore scrubs that were tailored in a way that spoke of competence and authority— but the warmth in her smile softened the edge, making the hurried chaos of the ED feel just a little less overwhelming.

"My name is Lyn," the nurse introduced herself as they walked. "I'm just going to grab your vitals, take some history, and get a blood sample from you, okay?"

Jaida nodded, trying to anchor herself as she lowered into the vinyl chair in the small triage room. The leather was cool and slightly sticky under her palms.

Jaida sat still in the triage room, as Lyn moved efficiently, pulling out the sphygmomanometer, thermometer, and blood collection supplies with precise, practiced motions. The rhythmic click of caps being removed, the soft swish of gloves being pulled on—these small sounds were grounding, if only slightly, amid the distant hum of monitors and the low chatter of other nurses.

Another nurse peeked into the room, calling Lyn away for a moment. "Sorry, I'll be right back," Lyn said, stepping out.

Jaida's gaze drifted, and before she knew it, her mind had run miles away from the bright, sterile room.

The white of the Emergency Department pressed in around her and washed together in blinding, relentless white. No color. No texture. The monotony made her head spin, like staring at snow for too long. She closed her eyes, encouraging herself to find some respite from the sensory overload. But closing her eyes didn't bring peace. Instead, it unlocked a door she hadn't meant to open. Aaron.

Aaron and Jaida went way back—to high school. Just acquaintances then, exchanging the occasional nod, nothing more. Years later, a casual reconnection on Facebook—likes, comments, short messages—slowly evolved into a real friendship. They weren't seeking romance, but life has a way of rewriting boundaries.

Eventually, they started dating. Aaron had a son, a bright-eyed boy he adored. Jaida remembered the first time she met him at Chuck E. Cheese, the way Aaron beamed as she and his son laughed over arcade games, sharing pizza and ski-ball victories. She thought it was a milestone, a sign of something lasting. But shortly after, Aaron refused exclusivity. He gave her permission to date others—as long as he didn't hear about it.

The betrayal came quietly at first—he lied about New Year's Eve, his indifference slipping into controlling behavior. Then came the violence, the manipulation, the intrusion into her family life. Jaida's brother, loyal and protective, was dragged into arguments she hadn't asked to have, twisting truths in ways that left her isolated. The last time she was in the Emergency Department was because of the physical attack— the shove that sent her into the wall, the head injury, the broken thumb—it left her body and her trust fractured.

Her work as a nurse became a negotiation with pain: syringes, IVs, Foley catheters—all requiring precision she could barely manage. Coworkers offered support where they could, but every accommodation was temporary, fragile. Reporting the abuse wasn't an option—nurses couldn't afford the stigma, so she carried it alone.

Even forgiveness became a weapon she wielded against herself. She had apologized to Aaron, which felt like shards of glass being swallowed, as self-love and healing task. But the holes he left in her life—her heart, her family, her trust— remained, visible, unpatched. And now, sitting here, Jackson absent, it all came rushing back. She felt that same raw isolation, that same sense of abandonment that had haunted her for years.

Jaida hadn't noticed Lyn re-enter the room until she spoke. "Jaida?" Her voice was soft but carried authority, a thread pulling her back from the spiral.

Jaida's shoulders were tense, her body leaned forward, elbows on her knees, hand pressed to her mouth. She gave a small, fake smile. "I'm fine," she said, though the tremor in her chest betrayed her words.

Lyn crouched slightly, pushing her red hair behind her ear before placing a hand lightly on the back of Jaida's chair. "Hey, it's okay. Take a deep breath with me. Can you do that?"

Jaida nodded, forcing herself to focus. In through the nose for a count of four. Hold for four. Out through pursed lips, like slowly blowing out a candle. Hold for four. Repeat. Slowly, the tension in her shoulders eased, her racing heart began to steady, and she reminded herself—even here, even now—she could find a small measure of control.

She knew she couldn't live trapped in these spirals forever. Something had to give. Maybe it was courage she needed—courage to reclaim her own life, to rebuild what had been broken. For now, she clung to the rhythm of her breath, each inhale and exhale a tether to the present, a lifeline out of the storm.

No one would know by looking at her. But inside, Jaida was exhausted—bone-deep, quiet, the kind of tired that didn't fade with sleep. Still standing. Still beautiful. Still brave. But quietly, relentlessly drained.

Outwardly, she had her life together. Nearly five years into her nursing career, she floated between units at one of the most prestigious hospitals in the city. Her teal scrubs always pressed, her badge clipped perfectly to her chest, her hair pulled back just so—on paper, she was the embodiment of success.

She'd graduated with honors from a competitive bachelorette nursing program. Bought her first car at 25 and first home at 27. Everything was meticulously documented, a list of achievements that would impress anyone who glanced at her résumé.

It was her father, now gone, who had taught her what it meant to stand on her own. She could still feel the warmth of the garage on summer mornings, the rough wood of the workbench pressing into her small palms as he moved with steady purpose. The tang of motor oil and grease mingled with the lingering aroma of his Joop cologne, a scent so familiar it felt etched into her memory. His voice—deep, booming, impossible to ignore—filled the space, echoing off walls stacked with tools and bouncing in the corners of her mind.

"Jaida, don't depend on any man for anything! NOTHING!" he had barked once, fire in his eyes igniting a mixture of fear and awe in her chest. She had reached up, tracing the grooves of his wedding ring with her small fingers, memorizing the ridges as if they held the secret to his strength. When she had dared to raise an eyebrow, pointing out that he, too, was a man, he snapped back, "I'm your dad. It's my job to take care of you, but I want you to get to a place where you don't even feel the need to depend on me. Because one day I won't be here."

They had watched countless sunsets together from the porch, the sky melting in shades of tangerine, rose, and gold. She remembered leaning against him, her small hand brushing his sleeve, eyes wide as the horizon seemed to stretch forever. The fading light would sit on his bald scalp, and he would hum low, content tunes, the kind that felt like home.

Even now, decades later, she could feel the ache of those moments—the quiet beauty, the warmth, the sense of being held yet encouraged to stand tall.

Her fingers unconsciously brushed the necklace at her throat, cool metal a tether to him, to those sunsets, to his voice, to the lessons he had carved into her heart. She lifted her gaze toward the evening sky outside the window, tracing the streaks of light as if the sun itself might carry his guidance.

Her throat tightened, the familiar pull of grief pressing at her ribs, and her eyes stung, but she blinked the tears back, an old habit. Her hand rose to rest lightly over her chest, mimicking the small, protective gestures of her childhood self—anchoring her to memory, to the rhythm of love and loss she had always carried.

Even now, the ache was permanent, a shadow folded into her ribs. Yet somewhere beneath it, a steady pulse remained—her father's lessons, the strength he had instilled, and the quiet reminder that she could stand alone. Some loves never leave, and some sunsets never fade; they linger in the chest, in the hands, in the quiet bend of a neck lifted toward the sky.

She was admired—praised even. At 28, strangers often marveled that she wasn't married yet. No kids. No boyfriend. "A catch like you—your soulmate must be on the way," they'd say. She smiled, nodded, pretending to believe it. But inside, the truth was stark: she didn't feel whole.

Standing at five-foot-three, with sun-kissed golden-brown skin and long, natural dark hair cascading in gentle waves, Jaida drew attention effortlessly. Her hazel eyes, shifting with the sunlight to flecks of gold and green, held stories she rarely shared: of pain, endurance, and survival. Success, she knew, wasn't about what people saw—it was about what you felt. And happiness? That was still something she was chasing.

She had been doing the work—inner child healing, shadow work, breaking generational cycles. Her growth had come in uneven waves, through sweat, tears, and countless nights of journal entries. Her invisible scars were armor, her transformation forged not for beauty, but survival.

As Lyn resumed her tasks, Jaida tried to fix herself to the present, letting the nurse's calm and practiced rhythm offer a fragile tether. Lyn's hands moved efficiently, checking her vitals: the cuff inflating around her arm with a soft hiss, the thermometer beeping gently as it registered her temperature, the pulse oximeter casting its small green glow against her fingertip. Each beep, each click, each soft swish of medical supplies brought a strange sense of order to the chaos in Jaida's mind.

Lyn reached for a tray of equipment, lining up alcohol swabs, syringes, and tubes with meticulous care. As she ripped open the top of an alcohol wipe, a sharp, clean scent filled the small triage room, cutting through Jaida's swirling thoughts. She inhaled cautiously, letting the crisp, familiar tang of rubbing alcohol distract her for a moment.

Her hands rested lightly on the cool vinyl of the chair, as she noticed the subtle hum of the monitors around her, the soft clicking of Lyn's gloves as she snapped them on, and the faint swish of the nurse moving between supplies. Each motion, each sound, each sensory cue, formed a steady cadence she could follow, a tether to the present that reminded her she wasn't alone.

For a brief moment, she let herself breathe. Following the rhythm Lyn set—not the relentless, anxious cadence of her own thoughts, but the steady, deliberate one of someone whose presence said: *I've got this. You're in safe hands.*

Soon, the door to the triage area swung open again, and a female doctor entered. She carried herself with a calm authority, a tailored white lab coat draped over her scrubs, a stethoscope looped casually around her neck. Her dark hair was pulled into a neat bun, and her sharp eyes scanned the room with professional efficiency, softening slightly when they landed on Jaida.

After a quick exchange, the doctor typed notes into the computer mounted to the wall, her fingers flying across the keyboard. A prescription was entered; her instructions brief but clear. Jaida watched, taking in the subtle confidence in the doctor's posture, the tilt of her shoulders, the steady cadence of her voice.

And just like that, with the paperwork completed and the prescription in the system, Jaida was free to go. She exhaled, a small smile tugging at her lips, feeling the weight of the day shift slightly. For now, she could step away, even if just for a moment, from the chaos of the hospital—and from the storm she carried inside herself.

Jaida stood, brushing the sleeve of her scrub top over her hands, and turned to Lyn. "Thank you… for helping me calm down back there," she said softly, her voice a little raw but sincere.

Lyn offered a warm, understanding smile, her eyes gentle behind the mask. "You did all the hard work, Jaida. I just guided you a bit. You're stronger than you realize."

Jaida nodded, letting herself absorb the quiet reassurance. The tension in her shoulders eased, just a fraction, as she felt the weight of the storm inside her lift.

"Take care of yourself," Lyn added, her voice steady but kind, as she stepped aside to let Jaida pass.

Jaida stepped out of the triage room into the hospital corridor. The harsh white walls and fluorescent lights no longer felt oppressive. Instead, the soft, steady swish of a housekeeping mop against the tile in the waiting room reached her ears, accompanied by the low hum of distant monitors and rolling carts. The rhythmic sound of the present, replaced the chaos in her mind with something simple and predictable.

For a brief moment, she felt untethered from her own racing thoughts. Held instead by the small, ordinary rhythms of the hospital around her.

She paused at the automatic doors, feeling the cool air from the lobby brush against her face, and let herself take a full, deep breath.

She stepped outside, as the city waited with its usual indifferent rhythm. A distant horn blared, footsteps echoed softly on the pavement, and a faint breeze carried the mixed scent of exhaust and fallen leaves. Over it all, the wail of an approaching ambulance rose and fell, weaving through the urban hum like a reminder of lives in motion—urgency, crisis, and care intersecting in fleeting sound. For a moment, the chaos outside and the chaos inside her chest seemed to line up, allowing her to breathe, if only just enough to feel present.

And yet, the weight of the moment—the waiting, the anxiety, the memories—lingered, coiling behind her ribs like a shadow that refused to leave. Even as she drew in air, slow and deliberate, letting each inhale and exhale ground her in the present, she could feel the storm inside her, restless and patient, waiting for the next heartbeat to stir it.

Her hands tingled, a faint tremor she tried to hide, and the tightness in her chest pressed against her lungs with every careful breath. Her thoughts spun as she thought, *how did I get here?*

Chapter Three

Behind the Mask

Three months ago, Jaida stepped into the Annual All Black Masquerade Gala at the Grand Regent Hotel, and the world had seemed to shimmer around her.

Black velvet drapes lined the walls, soft as midnight, while silver candelabras flickered atop every table. Their flames fracturing against crystal glasses and scattering tiny galaxies across the polished marble floor. The scent of flowers and champagne wove through the air, mingling with the faint perfume of guests as laughter and whispered conversations floated over the low hum of a string quartet. The cello's rich, velvety notes wrapped around her like a warm shawl, while the violins danced above it, sharp and playful, chasing the light.

She moved slowly, letting her gloved fingers brush against the cool edge of a table, feeling the smoothness of polished silver under her touch. Every mask she passed seemed to carry a story: the subtle tilt of a head, a flash of gold filigree catching the chandelier light, a smile hidden beneath ornate lace. Crystal flutes chimed with every toast, the sound rising and falling like ripples on a dark lake. Even the marble underfoot seemed to hum, a muted echo of the gala's elegance.

Jaida's own mask pressed lightly against her skin, a reminder of the delicate boundary between herself and the spectacle. She inhaled, letting the scent of fresh flowers curl through her senses, and for a moment, she felt part of the night's magic—as though the room itself had paused to breathe with her, every flicker of light, every note of music, every subtle fragrance carrying the promise of possibility.

Jaida adjusted her feathered black mask, her fingers brushing over the delicate sequins that lined its edges. She wore a strapless black gown that hugged her curves before cascading into a soft, flowing train. The fabric shimmered subtly under the chandeliers, as if catching the light with every movement. A thin, silver belt cinched her waist, adding a touch of understated elegance to the ensemble. Her hair, styled in soft waves, fell to her shoulders, and a pair of teardrop diamond earrings completed the look.

Standing beside her, Monday Harris radiated confidence in a figure-hugging black gown that sparkled with tiny crystals.

"This is what I call a crowd," Monday said, tilting her crystal flute to her lips and letting the champagne sparkle on her tongue. Her gaze swept the ballroom, taking in the glittering sea of black gowns and sharply tailored tuxedos, the subtle flash of jeweled masks, the way candlelight fractured against crystal glasses like tiny, spinning galaxies.

She noticed the hush of whispered conversations, the slight tilt of heads leaning closer for secrets, the careful brush of gloves against satin as people passed. "Money, power, and secrets," she murmured, voice low, almost savoring the tension that hummed beneath the polished surface. "It's a cocktail waiting to spill."

Around her, laughter and the low hum of the string quartet wove together, wrapping the room in a gilded elegance that felt both intoxicating and fragile—like the finest crystal poised on the edge of a table.

Jaida smirked. "And here I thought we were just here for charity."

"Please" Monday snarked. "Charity's the front. People are here to show off, network, and maybe, if we're lucky, make a difference."

They approached the registration table, where a young attendant in a custom black vest and white gloves greeted them with a practiced smile. His name tag read *Event Staff*, and he moved with the smooth precision of someone who had done this hundreds of times—gesturing subtly toward the pens, handing out ballots with a gentle nod, and guiding guests along with a soft, polite explanation. "Once you've filled out your ballot, please place it in the box over there," he said, pointing to a sleek, black ballot box gleaming under the chandelier light. "The charity with the most votes will receive tonight's donation pot. Every vote counts, so make it meaningful."

Jaida's fingers brushed the smooth cardstock as she took her ballot, noting the careful alignment of papers and the gentle undercurrent of organization behind the poised exterior.

Around her, the ballroom buzzed softly while masked guests drifted past with elegant ease, laughter and whispered compliments punctuating the air.

Her eyes lingered on *The Melanie Lenora Foundation*, the elegant script standing out among the list of charities like a quiet promise waiting to be noticed. She glanced up at the attendant, whose practiced smile remained steady, a small anchor amid the glittering, intoxicating swirl of the gala.

"Looks like you've already decided," Monday remarked, watching Jaida quickly scrawl her vote.

"I've read about their work," Jaida said, sliding her ballot into the sleek black box, the smooth surface cool under her fingertips. "They help families dealing with terminal illnesses. It hits close to home."

Monday nodded slowly, her eyes softening as she followed the movement of the ballot, the faint glimmer of chandelier light catching the edges of her mask. She absently traced the rim of her crystal flute with a fingertip, a small, almost unconscious gesture that betrayed the tug of memory. "It's a good choice," she murmured, her voice quieter now, carrying a weight that made Jaida's chest tighten slightly—cousins, yes, but close enough that unspoken understanding passed between them in a glance. "I'll vote for them too" Monday stated as she completed the ballot selection.

"The focus on terminal illness... it DOES hit close to home," Monday admitted, a shadow of sadness brushing her features. Jaida noticed the small furrow in her brow, the brief catch in her breath, and the way her fingers brushed the thin chain of her bracelet as if seeking grounding. For a moment, a flicker of chandelier light caught the corner of Monday's mask just so, and she blinked, momentarily transported by the golden shimmer—like sunlight falling on a memory long held.

Her lips pressed into a thin line, eyes drifting to the soft reflections on the marble floor, as though remembering someone lost to that very struggle. Then, with a practiced lift of her chin and a small, wry smile—familiar and reassuring, like a shared family signal—she added, "Besides, the other options are mostly vanity projects."

Jaida gave Monday a quiet, understanding nod, and a tiny squeeze on her hand against her ballot. Feeling the unspoken bond that came with shared history and family ties, the weight of empathy passed silently between them as Monday slid her ballot into the sleek black box.

"Well, at least this is more exciting than Uncle Anthony's annual holiday party," Monday quipped, holding her champagne flute delicately between her fingers, the golden bubbles catching the chandelier light and winking like tiny stars. Her eyes sparkled behind her mask, and a faint smile tugged at the corners of her lips as she leaned slightly toward Jaida.

Jaida let out a soft chuckle, the sound mingling with the muted hum of conversation and the distant clink of crystal flutes around them. "Barely," she admitted, brushing a loose strand of hair behind her ear. "At least here, we get to feel like we're doing something worthwhile."

The two cousins clinked their glasses lightly, a gentle chime that punctuated their quiet camaraderie, and took a slow sip, letting the crisp, effervescent warmth of the champagne settle across their tongues.

With their ballots cast, they strolled into the heart of the ballroom, the smooth notes of the string quartet mingling with the subtle beat from the DJ in the corner, wrapping around them like a velvet ribbon of sound.

Waiters in crisp uniforms glided through the crowd, balancing trays of sparkling champagne and artfully crafted hors d'oeuvres, their polished movements keeping pace with the rhythm of the music. Around them, the soft tapping of heels on the polished marble echoed lightly, blending with the music to create a gentle, lively cadence that carried through the glittering space.

"Do you know who's running the foundation?" Monday asked, plucking a smoked salmon canapé from a passing tray.

"Jackson Williams," Jaida replied, her tone casual. "I hear he's... efficient, but I don't know much else. Probably some old, stuffy guy in a bowtie."

Monday shook her head slightly, a playful tilt to her lips as her fingers lightly tapped the stem of her champagne flute. "Let's hope he's not the one giving the winning speech tonight. Those types always drag on."

As they stepped into the mingling crowd, Jaida's attention was caught before she even saw him—a rich, smoky scent of Oud drifting through the air, warm and alluring, weaving around her senses like a magnetic pull. She inhaled almost instinctively, and when she turned, she saw him: a tall man in a black tuxedo that seemed sculpted for him. He stood about six-foot-one, his posture relaxed yet commanding, the kind that didn't demand attention but drew it effortlessly. His mask revealed piercing eyes that lingered on her with a quiet intensity.

The cologne clung subtly to his skin, smooth and sophisticated, lingering in the warm glow of the chandeliers. A fresh fade framed his face, dark brown waves brushed into precise, polished lines.

Every detail—the scent, the effortless stance, the watchful gaze—made Jaida's chest tighten with an unfamiliar thrill, her pulse quickening and her fingers brushing lightly against the edge of her mask as if anchoring herself to the moment.

But it was his eyes that truly unmoored her—deep brown at first, warm and steady, until the light shifted and flecks of green shimmered through, subtle yet impossible to ignore. They held a quiet curiosity, the kind of gaze that didn't just meet yours but seemed to trace the edges of who you were, pulling her in with an almost magnetic weight.

Jaida felt a faint shiver ripple down her spine, her breath catching for just a moment, and she found herself tilting her head slightly, as if leaning closer might somehow hold the pull of those eyes. Her fingers brushed against the edge of her mask almost unconsciously, while a flutter of warmth danced through her chest, betraying the quiet thrill of being seen so completely.

"Excuse me," he said, his deep voice cutting through the low hum of conversation in the room. "I couldn't help but notice your choice at the ballot box. The Melanie Lenora Foundation."

Jaida turned to face him fully, surprised by the directness of his approach. "Oh, yes. I know someone who was affected by a terminal illness. It's a cause worth supporting."

The man nodded, a shadow of emotion crossing his face as his lips curling into a bittersweet smile. "It's a cause close to my heart, too. My mother passed away from a terminal illness. The foundation's named in her honor."

Jaida's breath caught, her mind racing to connect the dots. The tailored suit, the commanding presence, the familiarity of his voice from interviews she'd seen. Jaida's eyes widened as the realization dawned. "Wait... you're not—"

"Jackson Williams," he said, offering his hand with a faint smile. "I am. And you are?"

"Jaida," she said, shaking his hand. Her voice faltered slightly while her heart sank as embarrassment bubbled within her. "I—wow, I didn't realize... I mean, I thought you might be, um, older or..." She trailed off, biting her lip.

Jackson's smile widened, and his eyes sparkled with amusement "Let me guess. You thought I was some gray-haired philanthropist in a bowtie, barking orders at my staff?"

Jaida admitted, wincing at how her earlier comments to Monday now felt. "I might have said as much to my cousin." Monday chuckled and took a sip of her champagne as she turned away and began to walk towards the bar for a refill.

Jackson's laugh was rich and unrestrained. "Don't worry, you're not the first to make that assumption I've been told I need to work on my public image."

Jaida managed a nervous chuckle, the warmth of his laughter disarming her. "Well, you're definitely not what I expected."

"Good to know," he replied, his tone lighter now. He tilted his head, his gaze warm. "But now that I've surprised you, how about I prove it to you over dinner sometime? No speeches or board meetings, just a chance to show you I'm not as stuffy as you imagined."

Jaida blinked again, her heartbeat quickening. "Are you asking me on a date, Mr. Williams?"

"I am," he replied smoothly. "And I promise, no speeches or business talk—just good food and a chance to get to know the woman who wasn't afraid to tell me I seemed boring."

Her laughter bubbled up, easing the tension. "Well, when you put it that way, how could I say no?"

"Good. It's a date."

As Jackson excused himself to prepare for his speech, Jaida watched him walk away, her mind spinning. She'd come to the gala to support a cause, but she hadn't expected to meet the man behind it—or to agree to a date with him.

Monday reappeared at her side, her eyes sparkling with curiosity. "Well, well. Someone caught the attention of *the* Jackson Williams. That was unexpected. I leave you alone for two minutes, and you're already charming the city's most eligible bachelor. Girl, what did I miss?"

Jaida shook her head, still processing. "Just... the start of something I didn't see coming. I didn't even know who he was at first. And now... he asked me out."

Monday raised her glass with a knowing smile. "Here's to surprises. Now let's see if his speech lives up to the man himself."

Jaida couldn't help but smile as she clinked glasses with Monday then took a sip of her own champagne. The evening was unfolding in ways she never could have predicted.

The whir of conversation gradually quieted as the ballroom lights dimmed, leaving the chandeliers glowing like a constellation against the high ceiling. A soft chime echoed through the room, signaling the evening's next moment. Guests instinctively turned toward the stage where a sleek black podium stood adorned with the gold crest of the hotel.

Monday leaned in close to Jaida, whispering, "Here comes the boring part. Brace yourself."

But Jaida's attention was already fixed on the man who stepped into the spotlight. Jackson Williams.

He carried himself with effortless poise, his tuxedo sharp and commanding, his mask removed now that formality had begun. The lights caught his features—strong, composed, yet softened by something more vulnerable as he approached the microphone.

"Good evening," Jackson began, his deep voice filling the space with calm authority. "Thank you for being here tonight. The Annual All Black Masquerade Gala is more than a tradition—it is a reminder of what we can accomplish together when generosity leads the way."

Polite applause rippled across the room. Jaida's pulse quickened. She had just been speaking with him moments ago, laughing over her slip of the tongue, and now here he was—commanding the attention of a hundred guests.

Jackson's gaze swept the room, then settled with intention. "The Melanie Lenora Foundation was named in honor of my mother, Melanie. She was extraordinary, graceful, compassionate, full of life. She was diagnosed with a terminal form of cancer. As a kid, you don't understand what words like 'terminal' mean. All I knew was that the strongest person I had ever known suddenly couldn't get out of bed."

A hush fell over the crowd. Even the waitstaff paused, trays hovering midair.

Jackson's jaw tightened slightly, but his voice carried steady warmth. "I watched her fight, day after day, with courage that still inspires me. But what struck me most wasn't her illness—it was the silence around it. People didn't know how to talk about terminal illnesses. Families didn't know where to turn. And when she passed, I promised myself that her name would live on—not in grief, but in hope."

He paused, his eyes glistening under the light. Jaida felt her throat tighten; her heart caught in his words. This wasn't a corporate executive rattling off statistics. This was a son honoring his mother.

"That promise became this foundation," Jackson said, his voice full of pride and energy. "We exist to give families the resources my mother never had. We provide counseling, financial support, and—most importantly—community for those facing the toughest moments of their lives. Tonight, thanks to *your* votes, The Melanie Lenora Foundation has earned the honor of being the most supported organization. This is more than a win for us—it's a win for every mother, father, son, and daughter who needs someone to stand with them. Your belief in our mission gives us the power to reach even further, to touch more lives, and to make real, lasting change. From the bottom of our hearts, thank you for lifting this foundation—and the families we serve—higher than we ever imagined possible!"

The audience erupted in applause, many guests rising to their feet. Some dabbed at their eyes, moved by the raw honesty in his story.

Jaida clapped along, her own chest tightening. She had assumed the man behind the foundation was just another wealthy figurehead detached from the mission. But standing there, Jackson was anything but detached. He was personal. Genuine. Human.

Beside her, Monday whispered again, but her tone was softer now. "Okay... not boring."

Jaida's lips curved into the faintest smile. "Not at all."

Onstage, Jackson offered a final nod. "Thank you for being part of this night. Thank you for helping me keep my mother's memory alive. And thank you for believing that hope is stronger than despair".

The applause rose again, thundering now, echoing through the ballroom like waves crashing on shore.

As Jackson stepped down from the stage, the ballroom roared with applause that slowly melted into a hum of chatter. Guests were visibly moved—some leaning toward their companions in whispered admiration, others already discussing their votes with renewed conviction. The air felt different now, charged with something more than champagne and small talk.

Monday fanned herself dramatically with her program. "Well, I'll admit it—he had me misty-eyed. That was powerful."

Jaida nodded, still clapping absently. Her heart was heavy and light all at once. Heavy with the ache of his story, light with the strange pull she felt toward him. She hadn't expected to feel this stirred, this aware of him, beyond his title or wealth.

As Jackson moved through the crowd, guests stopped him at every turn. A senator in a black satin mask clapped him on the shoulder. A socialite in sequins pressed his hand between both of hers, whispering with reverence. He smiled graciously, but it was a smile honed from years of practice— warm, polished, professional.

But when his eyes found Jaida across the room, his smile shifted—something real flickered there. He excused himself from the small crowd, making his way toward her with purposeful strides.

"Oh boy," Monday muttered under her breath. "Here he comes. I'll just… disappear for a second." She glided off, leaving Jaida with her champagne glass clutched a little too tightly.

"Jaida," Jackson greeted when he reached her, his voice softer now, the stage command replaced with a more intimate warmth. "I hope I didn't bore you with all that."

She let out a quiet laugh, shaking her head. "Not at all. It was… moving. Honestly, I didn't expect to be so touched."

"I'm glad to hear that." His gaze lingered on her face, almost as if he were trying to read her thoughts. "I meant what I said earlier—I'd like to take you to dinner. But I realized I didn't ask how I can actually reach you."

Jaida's lips curved, her embarrassment from earlier returning in the form of a blush that crept across her cheeks. "That would make it hard to plan a date, wouldn't it?"

"Just a little," he teased, his eyes gleaming. "Unless you want me to track you down through the guest list."

She pulled her phone from the clutch at her side and glanced at Jackson. "Let me see your phone," she said with a mischievous grin, and when he handed it over, she tapped her number into it.

Holding her ringing phone up with a triumphant grin, she couldn't hide her excitement. "See? Verified. No wrong numbers, no excuses." As she handed Jackson his phone back, she added, "Now you don't have to stalk me through gala paperwork."

Jackson chuckled as he slipped his phone into his pocket, his eyes glinting with amusement.
"Perfect. Honestly, I had a feeling you wouldn't make it easy on me—you strike me as the type who'd hand me the wrong number just to see if I was clever enough to figure it out."

Jaida tilted her head, a sly smile tugging at her lips. "Maybe I would have," she teased, lifting her champagne glass. "But then again, if you weren't clever enough to figure it out, you probably wouldn't be worth the trouble."

Jackson's laughter came deep and genuine, his gaze dropping briefly to her phone before returning to her face. "Clever and cautious," he said, his voice warm with approval. "I like that. But you do realize you've just guaranteed I'll use it, right? No dodging my calls, Jaida."

Her lips curved into a smile, her eyes glimmering with mischief. "Who says I'd want to dodge them?"

For a moment, the world around them blurred—just the two of them standing in the middle of a glittering ballroom, their laughter and connection quietly stitched into the evening's grandeur.

Then another board member called Jackson's name, reminding him of his duties. He gave Jaida one last smile. "I'll be in touch, Jaida. Soon."

And with that, he disappeared once more into the swirl of guests, leaving her with a racing heart and the lingering promise of what was to come.

Monday returned at Jaida's side, grinning like a cat with a secret. "So… when's the date?"

Jaida rolled her eyes, but her smile gave her away.

Chapter Four

Tasting Something New

By the time Jackson finally set his coffee mug down, the city outside had settled, its earlier rush softening at the edges. He could have spent the morning unwinding, reviewing the foundation's next grant proposal, or catching up on emails—but something else tugged at him. He thought of Jaida.

Not the gala, not the brief exchanges, but *her*—the way she moved through the room, calm yet commanding, the spark in her eyes when she spoke, the way she had smiled at him that night. He had asked himself over and over whether it was reckless, whether it crossed some invisible boundary—but the thought of waiting, of sending a text that could never carry the weight of what he wanted to say, felt hollow. He wanted her to see, to hear, to know that he was sincere.

The drive to the hospital was quiet, meditative even. Sunlit building blurred past, and he let himself run through the words he would say, the way he would ask again—this time in person. Every red light, every turn, only heightened the anticipation, sharpening the edge of nervous excitement he hadn't felt in years.

He parked in the hospital garage, took a deep breath, and walked through the lobby, careful but deliberate. By the time he reached the end of the nursing unit's hallway, leaning casually against the fire door, he was calm, composed, but utterly aware of the risk he was taking. He was about to step into someone's world—their routine, their space—and hope it was received the way he intended.

And then he saw her. Jaida. At the nurse's station, badge clipped neatly to her scrubs, hair pulled back with meticulous care. The spark he remembered from the gala was still there—bright, alive—but now it was edged with surprise and curiosity, a current that made the air between them electric.

He straightened, one hand settling casually into the pocket of his slacks, the other relaxed at his side, and with a smile that balanced apology and intention, he spoke her name.

Time slowed.

Jaida's day had begun like any other—back-to-back admissions, endless charting, and the constant hum of hallway chatter that never seemed to pause. As a nurse in one of the city's busiest hospitals, unpredictability was her routine. Still, nothing—no patient, no call, no emergency— had prepared her for this.

When Jaida looked up and saw Jackson Williams standing at the end of the hallway of the nursing unit, time stuttered. The way he leaned casually against the fire door's frame, suggested that he'd come straight from the office. His sleeves were rolled neatly to his forearms, the crisp white of his dress shirt bright against his brown skin. Polished black oxfords gleamed beneath him, the kind of shoes that didn't belong in a hospital corridor but somehow made him stand out even more.

And that smile—sharp, warm, impossible to forget—was the same one she remembered from the Gala one week ago.

As she walked toward him, the steady beeps of telemetry monitors and the distant whoosh of an elevator filled the quiet between them. A few nurses glanced over—because men like Jackson didn't just appear on a floor like this without causing a ripple.

She stopped a few feet from him, crossing her arms—not defensive, but definitely curious.

"Okay," she said slowly, "how did you even know where I work? And how did you know I was on *this* unit today?"

Jackson's smile widened, something playful flickering in his eyes. "I have my ways," he said smoothly.

She raised a brow. "Your ways, huh?"

He shifted slightly, the fabric of his slacks catching the fluorescent light as he leaned in, speaking low enough that the words belonged only to her.

"Let's just say..." His voice lowered, warm and confidential. "When a man really wants to see someone again, he finds the right people to ask."

Jaida blinked. He wasn't even trying to hide it—he'd asked someone. Someone at *her* hospital.
"So you talked to somebody here?" she asked, half incredulous, half flattered.

He didn't deny it. "I might've," he replied, lips curving. "I'm resourceful."

Her pulse kicked up, uninvited and immediate. No one had ever shown up for her like that—not with intention, not with confidence, not with that kind of quiet boldness. And standing there, in her scrubs and badge and sensible shoes, she felt suddenly seen in a way she hadn't expected.

Her pulse kicked harder, impossible to hide, but she forced her face into composure. Her lips pressed into a measured line as she lifted her chin. "Mr. Williams," she said evenly, one brow arching in quiet reproach. Inside, though, her thoughts were anything but even. *He really came here? To the hospital? To my floor?*

Part of her wanted to be irritated, this was her workplace, her territory. But a deeper part, a softer part she didn't often indulge, warmed at the idea that he wanted to see her badly enough to track her down. It was bold. Too bold. And yet… it made something flutter pleasantly in her chest.

Jackson's smile softened, the edges losing their confident brightness. Something like guilt flickered in his eyes. "I know," he admitted, stepping closer—not enough to invade, but close enough that she could smell the faint trace of his cologne, clean and expensive. His voice dropped to a low, steady register. "I should've called. Texted, at least. You gave me your number, and I left you waiting."

Her throat tightened, a reaction she refused to let show on her face.

He paused, his gaze locking firmly onto hers, letting the moment stretch. "But I couldn't bring myself to do it. Sending words through a screen felt too impersonal. Too small for what I wanted to say. I needed to see you in person, so you'd know I was sincere when I asked again."

Her stomach fluttered before she could stop it. Her folded arms loosened, dropping from defense to intrigue. The irritation she'd tucked behind professionalism eased under the weight of his honesty. "I was beginning to think you'd lost interest," she said quietly, searching his face. "But you wanted to make me wait?"

He shook his head slowly. "No. I wasn't trying to make you wait. I wanted you to anticipate." His voice warmed, sincerity threading through every word. "I was trying to make sure I showed up the right way. And seeing you here... it felt right."

Her heartbeat thudded again—betrayal or possibility, she couldn't tell.

His eyes glinted with warmth. "Dinner. Tonight. Eight o'clock. A little Mexican spot I love. Say yes."

A reluctant smile tugged at her mouth. "You're nothing if not persistent, huh?"

"Relentless," he corrected smoothly. "And I promise—it'll be worth it."

Against her better judgment, she found herself nodding. "Eight o'clock."

Jackson's grin widened, satisfaction tempered with something tender. "Then I'll see you there." His voice dipped, a quiet velvet edge to it. "And Jaida—thank you for not giving up on me just yet."

The way he said her name left a warmth in her chest long after he disappeared from the unit.

When Jaida finally turned away from the fire door and started back toward the nurses station, she immediately felt eyes on her. Two of the day-shift nurses were openly watching, trying—and failing—to hide their smirks behind their computer monitors. Another leaned toward her coworker, whispering something that made them both snicker.

Jaida lifted her chart a little higher, pretending not to notice the chorus of knowing looks trailing her. But the heat rising in her cheeks gave her away. Every step back down the hallway echoed with the unspoken commentary radiating from her coworkers: *Girl... who was THAT?*

She kept her expression composed, professional even—at least until she slipped behind the station, where one of the nurses was already raising her brows like she expected a full report.

Jaida set the chart down on the counter with clinical precision, as if the steady placement of paper could anchor her heartbeat. She typed her notes into the computer a little too intently, hoping the movement would look routine enough to discourage commentary.

It didn't work. She could still feel the nurses' eyes on her, the quiet giggles, the exchanged glances. She kept her face neutral—borderline bored—as if handsome men in tailored slacks showed up on her unit every Tuesday.

But inside? Inside she was a complete mess.

Her pulse hadn't settled. Her hands weren't trembling, but they wanted to. A warmth curled in her stomach, refusing to fade, no matter how many patient notes she pretended to focus on.

Because the truth was embarrassing in its simplicity:
She liked what he did. She liked that he'd come all the way there. That he'd asked around. That he'd cared enough to show up himself instead of sending a text. Bold. Unreasonable. A little over-the-top. And undeniably flattering.

She took a slow breath, trying to school her expression back into something calm and unimpressed, but even she could feel the faint smile tugging at the corner of her mouth.

"Get it together," she murmured under her breath, clicking into the next patient chart. But her heart wasn't listening.

By the time Jaida's shift finally ended, she felt wrung out—not by the patients, but by the relentless teasing from her coworkers. Every time she passed the nurses' station, someone had wiggled their brows, whispered dramatically, or burst into suspiciously timed laughter.

So when the elevator doors slid shut behind her, sealing her away from the unit, she let out a breath she'd been holding for hours. The soft, rhythmic pulse of the elevator felt like relief itself. No eyes on her. No sly grins. No whispered "girl, he came all the way up here for YOU?"

Just silence. Blessed, grounding silence.

Outside, the cool evening air brushed against her cheeks. The sky was streaked in purples and blues, the hospital's lights glowing against the fading day. As soon as she slid into her car, she sank into the seat like she'd been carrying the entire unit on her shoulders.

But then the memory slipped in—Jackson leaning against the door frame, the warmth in his voice, the way he said her name like it was something worth coming for. And suddenly… that flutter in her chest returned.

She pulled out of the parking lot, tires gliding along the road. The city lights blinked past her window as anticipation slowly unfurled in her stomach, warm and steady. She shouldn't be this excited—not after one meeting and a bold visit—but she was. She absolutely was.

Her phone buzzed through her Bluetooth, lighting up the display. Monday.

Jaida hit the answer button on her steering wheel. "Hey," she said, trying—and failing—to sound casual.

"Girl," Monday's voice came through instantly, sharp and ready. "Why did I just see your text about some man *showing up at your job*? Explain. Immediately."

Jaida chuckled. "I knew you were going to call as soon as you read it."

"You're damn right I did. Start talking. Who is he, why was he there, and why does your voice sound like you're smiling?"

Jaida bit her lip, staring at the traffic as she turned onto the freeway. "It's Jackson. From the Gala."

"THE foundation guy? The fine one? Tall, coffee with the perfect amount of cream, shoulders like he hugs for a living—him?"

Jaida's eyebrows bowed in confusion. "That's... a weird description, but yes."

Monday practically squealed into the speaker. "Oh my goodness, so what happened?!"

Jaida took a breath, causing her eyebrows to relax, still half in disbelief. "He showed up on my unit. Like... walked onto the floor. Looking for me."

"I'm sorry, what?" Monday gasped. "At your job? Not outside? Not the lobby? THE ACTUAL UNIT?"

"Exactly. He asked around to figure out where I was assigned today."

Monday made a sound somewhere between delight and scandal. "Oh, he bold-bold. I LIKE him."

"Monday..."

"No, Jaida. Stop. I know that tone. You liked it."

Jaida hesitated—for all of two seconds. "...Yeah," she whispered. "Yeah, I did."

A dramatic gasp exploded through the speakers.
"OH! My gosh. My friend is blushing. Tell me everything."

Jaida recounted the whole encounter—the rolled-up sleeves, the hand in his pocket, the smooth apology, the way he said her name, the sincerity in his eyes. Monday ooh'd and ahh'd at all the right places.

By the time Jaida turned onto her street, Monday was practically vibrating. "So when's the date?" she demanded.

"Tonight," Jaida admitted.

"Oh, you were just going to drop that in at the END of the conversation?! Jaida! What are you going to wear?"

"I have absolutely no idea," Jaida said, pulling into her driveway. "I just got home."

"Oh, so we need to build a look. Let's get inside so I can mentally scan your closet."

"Monday, you are too much and it's ridiculous." Jaida laughed as she grabbed her bag and walked toward her front door.

"I do my best. Now hurry up."

Jaida unlocked the door, flicked on the lights, and kicked off her work shoes with a sigh of freedom.
"Okay," she said, stepping into her bedroom, phone still perched between her shoulder and ear. "I'm in my room."

"And what are we working with? Casual chic? Soft glam? Something with a slit? What's the assignment?"

"I don't know yet," Jaida admitted, glancing at her closet like it held all the answers. "I need to figure out the vibe."

"Well call me when you settle on your personality for the evening," Monday teased. "I want updates."

"Goodbye, Monday."

"Have fun on your date," Monday sang. "And Jaida?"

"Yeah?"

"Don't downplay this one. Something about him feels different."

The call clicked off, leaving the room quiet. Jaida exhaled, standing alone in the soft glow of her bedroom lamp, the weight of the night settling over her—warm, electric, thrilling.

It was time to get ready. Time to choose something to wear. Time to see what this could become.

Later that evening, Jaida stood outside the vibrant glow of the Mexican restaurant, smoothing the front of her flowy white blouse. Paired with high-waisted jeans and tan sandals. She looked effortlessly casual, though her heartbeat betrayed the effort she'd put into the simple look. Her hair, loosely braided over one shoulder, caught the light of the neon sign above her, and she tugged at it absentmindedly until a familiar voice broke through the hum of the city street.

"You're right on time," Jackson said as he approached, dressed in dark jeans and a pale blue button-up with the sleeves rolled to his elbows. Relaxed, confident, devastatingly handsome.

"Of course," she said, teasing to cover her nerves. "Punctuality is important."

"Noted," he said, holding the door open. "I'll make sure to arrive fifteen minutes early next time, just to impress you."

She laughed softly as she stepped past him. "You might want to work on just showing up first."

"Then I'll have to remember that" he murmured, holding the door for her as they stepped into a swirl of aromas—charred peppers, sizzling meat, the citrus bite of fresh lime. Mariachi music flowed from speakers tucked in the corners, blending with the laughter and chatter of diners packed into colorful booths.

They were seated near a window, a cozy two-top draped in a bright woven cloth. Jaida ordered a passionfruit margarita, Jackson, a classic lime. When the oversized sugar-rimmed glasses arrived, condensation dripping, their first sips were cool relief from the warmth of the evening.

Jackson raised his glass slightly. "To second chances—earned, not assumed."

Jaida's lips curved as she met his toast. "And to actually following through this time."

Dinner arrived in a sizzling procession: steak, chicken, and shrimp fajitas laid out with steaming tortillas, cilantro-lime rice, pico de gallo, sour cream, and guacamole so fresh it made her mouth water.

Jaida laughed outright as Jackson fumbled with his tortilla, guacamole slipping out the side. "You're hopeless," she teased, reaching for her own.

"I'm great at foundations," he countered with mock offense, gesturing with his tortilla. "Clearly just not fajitas."

"Clearly," she said, chuckling. "Maybe next time, I'll order you a burrito. Pre-rolled."

He leaned in slightly, eyes warm with amusement. "Next time, huh? I like the sound of that."

Her pulse fluttered. "Don't push your luck."

"Oh, I intend to," he said, grin widening.

Her laughter bubbled over, real and unguarded, and it set something alight in him.

Their conversation flowed easily, shifting from work stories to old travel memories. Jaida spoke about her patients—their resilience, the way they find joy in even the smallest things. Jackson listened intently, genuinely engaged.

"You light up when you talk about them," he said. "It's...nice to see."

Jaida tilted her head a bit caught off guard by the softness in his tone. "They remind me why I do what I do. It's easy to forget the heart behind the job when you're buried under paperwork."

Jackson nodded knowingly. "I get that. My foundation started as a project for my mom, but it has become a piece of me. She passed a few years ago."

Her expression softened. "I'm so sorry. You must miss her."

"I do," he said quietly. "She had this way of making everything feel okay. Even when it wasn't. Every big decision I make, I still hear her voice in my head— *'Make it count, Jackson'*." He smiled faintly, then exhaled. "So I try."

Jaida reached out, her hand brushing his briefly. "She'd be proud. You carry her with you, even here."

Between bites and margarita refills, conversation began to unravel the layers between them. They spoke of light things first—favorite foods, embarrassing stories from college. But soon, Jackson's tone shifted.

"My mother loved food like this," he said suddenly, gaze drifting toward the flickering candles between them. "She used to make tamales every Christmas Eve. The kitchen would be chaos—flour everywhere, cousins sneaking bites before they were done." He smiled faintly, but there was a heaviness beneath it. "There hasn't been a Christmas the same since she passed."

Jaida's chest tightened at the rawness in his voice. "I'm sorry," she said softly. "It sounds like she left a lot of warmth behind, though. The kind that doesn't fade."

"She did," he agreed, voice thickening before he cleared his throat and forced a smile. "I like to think she'd be proud of the man I'm becoming."

He looked at her, eyes lingering. "Maybe that's why I didn't want to text," he said softly. "My mom always told me— 'if someone matters, show up.'"

The silence that followed was comfortable, charged. Then Jaida smiled lightly, breaking it before it grew too heavy. "I think she'd approve of tonight's effort."

He chuckled. "I'm glad to hear that." He looked down for a moment, "My dad and I", he paused then back at her with a hint of hesitancy in his gaze. "We haven't really talked much since she passed."

Jaida tilted her head, her tone gentle but firm. "Jackson...don't let too much time pass. Tomorrow isn't promised. Sometimes we wait for the right moment, and it never comes. You should reach out before it's too late."

He let her words hang in the air for a moment, staring at his margarita, swirling it slowly. Finally, he met her eyes again. "Yeah...maybe you're right." His voice was softer now, reflective. "I've been avoiding it, I guess. But...maybe I should."

Jaida smiled lightly, warmth in her eyes. "It's never too late to start."

He gave a small nod, a faint smile tugging at his lips. "Never too late," he agreed, and just for a heartbeat, the tension between them softened into something quieter, more intimate.

To balance the weight of the moment, Jaida shifted the focus. "My parents are both still alive. And very much involved in my life—sometimes too much," she added with a grin. "My dad, especially. We're close. He's...steady. The kind of man who's always there when I need him."

Jackson laughed. "Sounds like a good man."

"He is," she said fondly. "I'm planning to surprise him soon actually. I want his help house hunting. My cousin, a different cousin than the one from the Gala, is a realtor, and she's been nagging me to start looking. I just haven't told him yet. He'll be thrilled."

"He's going to love that," Jackson said, smiling. "And let me guess—you're going to pretend you need his advice just so he feels useful."

"Exactly," she said, grinning. "You get it."

"Oh, I've met enough dads to know how the game works."

Their laughter came easily, bouncing between them, the rhythm of two people falling into step with each other without realizing it.

Conversation lingered late into the night, the restaurant gradually emptying around them.

By the time their plates were cleared and the last of the margaritas gone, the restaurant had thinned out. The candles had burned low, and the easy warmth between them had deepened into something slower, something that lingered.

The night air outside was thick with the scent of blooming flowers, the faint drift of traffic carrying in from the city beyond. Jackson walked beside her to her car, his hands tucked into his pockets, his stride unhurried.

"You were right," Jaida said, breaking the silence. "Dinner was worth it."

He looked at her with a quiet smile. "You make it sound like you doubted me."

"Oh, I did," she said, laughing softly. "But you've made a decent comeback."

"I'll take decent," he murmured, stepping a little closer. "For now."

Her breath caught at the subtle promise in his tone. At her car door, he paused, tilting his head slightly as he looked at her. "Thank you," he said, voice low. "For giving me another chance to do this the right way. Tonight was...better than I imagined."

Her smile was shy but certain. "I'm glad I came."

He stepped a fraction closer, sandalwood and something warm enveloping her senses. For a moment, the world narrowed to the space between them. He didn't press, didn't push—just pulled her into a warm embrace that lingered long enough to make her pulse quicken. Her cheek brushed against his chest, his breath stirring the loose braid over her shoulder.

"Goodnight, Jaida," he murmured against her temple.

"Goodnight, Jackson," she whispered back, reluctant as she pulled away.

When she slid into her car and started the engine, her hands trembled just slightly on the steering wheel. She hadn't felt this way in a long time—drawn in, but steady. Curious, but cautious.

As she drove home, her fingers tapped the steering wheel in rhythm with her racing heart. It had been a long time since she'd felt this—hope, excitement, the beginnings of something that could be more.

And though she tried to temper her thoughts, a smile curved her lips all the same. She found herself hoping, quietly but fervently, that this was just the beginning. And for the first time in a long while, new felt good.

Chapter Five

The Quiet Between Us

The night was quiet enough for Jackson to hear the soft hum of his refrigerator from the living room. It was the kind of silence that didn't bother him anymore — he'd grown used to it, almost found comfort in it.

Still, some nights, like this one, it pressed too close. He leaned back against the couch, thumb idly scrolling through the same text thread with his dad he hadn't responded to in weeks.

> **Dad:** Dinner Sunday? Just the two of us.

> **Dad:** Made your favorite last weekend. You'd better come before I eat all the leftovers.

> **Dad:** Call me when you can, son.

Jackson sighed, tossing the phone onto the cushion beside him. The guilt didn't sting anymore — it just sat there, heavy and dull, like something he'd learned to carry without feeling. His father meant well. Always had. But lately, even a simple dinner invitation felt like too much.

This time of year always pressed hardest on Jackson, settling into him with a familiar heaviness he'd learned to carry but never quite learned to escape.

The annual gala was successful event, another night of shaking hands, giving speeches, smiling just enough to keep anyone from asking questions. He always scheduled it during this season, right around the anniversary of his mother's passing.

Keeping himself busy helped. Filling the calendar, filling the room, filling the silence. It made the grief feel contained, manageable, as if the noise and movement could drown out the ache.

But now, alone at home, nothing shielded him. The timing of the gala hadn't saved him from the pull of the season. It had only delayed the moment, grief found him again.

He got up and crossed the room, flicking off the lamp. The city outside was quiet, the streetlights stretching long shadows across his apartment floor.

On the shelf near the TV sat a framed photo of his mother — laughing, her head tilted slightly back, sunlight touching her face. The picture had been taken the year before she got sick. He hadn't meant to look at it tonight, but now he couldn't look away.

When she died, it was like someone turned the volume down on the world. The days after her funeral blurred into weeks — people bringing casseroles, sending texts, checking in. Then they stopped. Everyone else's life went on. His didn't.

He created and threw himself into work at the Foundation. His team kept saying they admired his focus, his drive, how he turned grief into purpose. But they didn't know that he wasn't driven — he was hiding. Building something gave him control. The ache didn't touch him when he was busy saving someone else.

His father never understood that. Or maybe he did, and that was the problem.

When the phone rang that first week, Jackson had let it go to voicemail. Then again the next day. And again. By the third week, he stopped checking the missed calls. It wasn't that he didn't care. It was that every time he heard his father's voice, it made the loss feel real again.

He'd grown up watching how deeply his father loved his mother — the way he'd always held her hand when they walked together, even after twenty years. They were quiet people, not flashy or overly affectionate, but the love was there in the small things — her cooking for him, his habit of checking the locks twice before bed because she always forgot.

When she died, his father broke in a way that scared him. There were days Jackson had gone over just to make sure the man was eating, but it never lasted. His father would start talking about her — her smile, her voice, the things she said the last night in the hospital — and Jackson would shut down. He couldn't sit through it. Couldn't breathe through it. So, he'd gone back to work.

He picked up the picture frame and traced the edge with his thumb, his chest tightening with that old familiar ache. There were things he never said to her. Words he thought he'd have time for later — *thank you, I love you, I'm proud to be your son.*

The voicemail icon blinked on his phone, a tiny red dot that felt louder than any sound in the apartment.

He sat back down and pressed play.

"Hey, son. I, uh… I know you're busy. I don't want to bother you. I just—". A pause. The sound of his father clearing his throat. "I miss her too. Every day. But I can't… I can't lose you too, Jackson. I know we haven't talked much lately, but I'm still here. You don't have to do this alone, okay?" Another pause. Softer this time. "Anyway. I love you, son. That's all."

Jackson exhaled slowly, eyes burning. He leaned forward, elbows on his knees, letting the weight of the message settle into him. His father's voice sounded older than he remembered — thinner somehow, like grief had worn it down.

He didn't call back. Not because he didn't care. Not because he was angry. He just didn't know what to say that wouldn't crack something open inside him.

He stood and poured himself a glass of water, staring out the window at the quiet city below. The lights blurred, soft and distant, like the world was still moving but he was stuck behind the glass. The water sat untouched on the counter.

His father wasn't losing him. Not really. He loved him. But love didn't always come with words. Sometimes it came in silence — in the stubborn way he kept working, in the steady way he carried his mother's memory like a secret inside him.

That was how he grieved. Quietly. Alone. The memory hit him suddenly, unbidden, as if the quiet of the apartment had peeled back the layers of time. The day of her funeral.

He remembered the drive to the cemetery, the air heavy and cool, the city strangely empty in the early morning. His father had driven, hands gripping the wheel like he might crumble if he let go. Jackson sat in the passenger seat, staring out the window at the rows of houses, each one ordinary, alive, oblivious to the world shifting under them.

At the service, people moved around them in clusters, offering condolences, nodding politely. He had smiled when necessary, muttered the right words. But inside, everything felt muffled, distant — like he was watching himself from underwater. His father had stood next to him, posture rigid, jaw tight, eyes occasionally meeting his. Neither spoke.

Afterwards, they had gone back to the house, and Jackson's father had tried. A small attempt: a joke about how she always left the kitchen a mess, the casserole she'd made the week before still sitting in the fridge. But the sound of it, meant to comfort, made Jackson flinch. Humor didn't fit in grief like this.

He remembered the silence that stretched between them at the kitchen table. The sunlight streaming through the blinds fell in harsh lines across the plates, cutting across the tension.

His father picked at his food, eyes flicking up occasionally, as if waiting for Jackson to say something. But Jackson couldn't. Words felt like betrayal — like admitting just how hollow the world had become.

He had left early that day, promising to come back another time. His father had said nothing, just nodded, the faintest crease of worry etched between his brows.

Weeks later, the messages came. Not from friends, not from colleagues — from his father. Brief texts. Short emails. A voicemail here and there. Jackson ignored most of them, some he deleted before listening, others he left in the inbox, a silent reminder of the world outside his self-made bubble.

One evening, he had gone home after a long day at the Foundation. The drive was quiet, music off, only the hum of tires on asphalt to mark the passage of time. Opening the door, he was hit with the faint scent of her — vanilla, lingering, comforting, impossible. He froze, heart tight.

The house looked the same. Plates on the counter, the table set for two, even though one chair had been empty for weeks. And there, sitting in her favorite chair, was his father. Eyes tired, but alive.

"Jackson," his father said softly.

Jackson hadn't moved yet. Just stood there in the doorway, the weight of his own grief pressing on him. "Hey," he managed finally, voice low.

Dinner was quiet, punctuated only by the clinking of cutlery. His father tried to fill the space with small talk — the news, a project at the Foundation, a neighbor's dog — but Jackson heard only the gaps. The unspoken words hung between them.

"You know," his father said finally, pausing, "she would've wanted us to… talk. To… not let it sit like this."

Jackson swallowed, staring at his plate. "I'm… fine," he said, more harshly than he intended.

His father exhaled, not pushing further. He had learned to let Jackson take his time. But it hurt anyway. "I know," he said. "I just… feel like I'm losing you too."

The words hit harder than Jackson expected. He wanted to respond, to reassure, to bridge the gap. But he didn't know how. So, he finished the meal, left the dishes, and walked out into the evening, telling himself that love could survive silence — that grief could be endured alone.

He drove back to the apartment, stomach tight, chest heavier than it had been all day. The voicemail from his dad that night blinked red in the corner of his phone. He listened, feeling the tremor in his father's voice, the quiet pleading for connection.

"Son, I don't want to lose you. I can't fix what's happened, I can't bring her back, but I don't want to lose you too. Call me when you're ready. I'm here. Always."

Jackson exhaled slowly, letting the weight of it settle. He didn't call back. Not yet. He wasn't walking away. He was just… not ready. Not ready to be vulnerable.

Instead, he poured himself a glass of whiskey, sat by the window, and watched the city breathe beneath him. In the distance, lights flickered. Somewhere, life moved forward. He stayed rooted in his grief, holding it close, carrying it like a secret no one could touch.

Even then, he loved his father. Always. But love didn't always need words. Sometimes, it existed in endurance, in quiet presence, in the stubborn refusal to let go even when he felt fractured inside.

And maybe — someday — he would learn how to let that love breathe without fear.

The apartment was dark except for the faint glow of the streetlights outside. Jackson sat cross-legged on the floor, the whiskey untouched at his side. His mother's picture leaned against the bookshelf, her eyes catching the light from the window, as if she were watching him.

He didn't know when the tears started. One moment he was staring at the skyline, the next he was pressed against the cold floor, letting it cool the heat of his tears. His hands gripping his knees, chest tight with the weight he'd carried for months. The grief he had kept neatly compartmentalized — around work, obligations, even the gala— had found him.

Memories pressed in, sharp and relentless. Her laughter echoing in the kitchen. The softness of her voice calling his name when he was a child. The way she used to brush her hand across his hair when he was sick. The mundane moments that now felt sacred.

His body ached—his heart ached—and he realized, with a raw, piercing clarity, just how much he had buried. But now, alone, it spilled out uncontrolled, a tidal wave of pain, longing, and love he couldn't put into words.

He let himself fall apart, truly, allowing the tears to soak his cheeks, shoulders, and hands. The sobs were quiet at first, then ragged, shaking his whole frame, but he didn't stop them. He didn't hide them. For the first time in a long while, Jackson simply *was*—broken, raw, human—letting the weight of his mother's absence press fully into him.

He remembered the night she got sick. The quiet in the hospital room, the beeping of machines filling the empty space, the way she reached for his hand even when it hurt her to move. He had tried to stay strong, to offer comfort, but it had always been him needing it, not her.

He thought of his father — how he had tried, silently, to hold the family together. How he still tried. The voicemails left unanswered, the texts ignored, the quiet invitations to dinners and talks that Jackson refused.

"I don't want to lose you too."

The words echoed in his mind. His father wasn't angry. He wasn't pushing. He just wanted connection. And Jackson had been too afraid, too raw, to give it.

He pressed his palms to his eyes, inhaling deeply, trying to ground himself in the present. He wasn't a child anymore. He wasn't helpless. But grief had a way of dragging even the strongest down, isolating him in ways he hadn't anticipated.

The memories blurred with reality. He could almost hear her in the apartment — humming softly while tidying up, her presence a comforting weight he could lean into. And he could almost hear his father's voice as well — calm, patient, waiting. Waiting for Jackson to realize that love didn't have to vanish with grief.

He thought of Jaida. Something about her had lingered with him after their first date — a warmth, a steadiness, a gentle resilience. He hadn't recognized it at the time, but now he understood why. She reminded him, in subtle ways, that grief could coexist with hope. That connection didn't have to be suffocating; it could be quiet, patient, enduring.

He closed his eyes and let himself imagine a conversation he wasn't ready to have yet. Words spilling out, raw and unfiltered. Confessions of loss, of anger, of love and regret.

His father listening, not judging, not rushing, just present. It was a fantasy, yes — but it was a seed. A small, fragile possibility.

He knew he wouldn't call tonight. Not yet. But tomorrow, maybe. Or the next day. He wasn't closing the door. He was just learning how to open it without breaking.

For now, he stayed on the floor, silent, breathing with the rhythm of the city outside. The weight of his grief was still there, but it didn't feel quite as suffocating.

Somewhere in the quiet, in the stillness, he felt the faintest stirrings of something he hadn't felt in months: the possibility that he could grieve and still be present. That he could love and still be strong.

He wasn't ready to speak. He wasn't ready to be vulnerable. But for the first time in a long time, he allowed himself to *feel* — to exist in the quiet, unguarded, in the company of memories and love he'd carried silently for so long.

And maybe, when the time was right, he would answer that voicemail.

But for now, he just breathed.

Chapter Six

Golden Moments

Time had a quiet way of moving when things finally started to feel right again.

Two months had passed since that afternoon Jackson showed up at Jaida's job with persistence in one hand and his unshakable calm in the other.

Since then, the two of them had slipped into a rhythm that felt... easy. Natural. Like they'd both been waiting for something they didn't know they needed.

Their days together became a collage of soft and spirited moments — dinners that stretched late into laughter, cooking classes where they battled playfully over whose pasta turned out better, and afternoons covered in clay from pottery and glass-blowing workshops.

When they weren't creating, they were exploring. One weekend, Jackson surprised her with an outdoor adventure at a nature park designed to inspire courage, connection, and discovery. They climbed, swung, and zipped through the trees, their laughter echoing through the canopy as they faced each challenge together.

Jaida remembered gripping the rope ladder, heart pounding, only to look down and see Jackson smiling up at her, steady and unshaken, reminding her she could do it.

It wasn't just the thrill of the adventure — it was how they learned each other in the process.

He saw how she overthought before she leapt, and she saw how he always led with quiet confidence.

She liked to plan; He liked to feel. Somewhere between the laughter, the teasing, and the long drives back home to her cozy townhouse, they started learning how the other moved through the world — and how, together, they made sense.

And Jaida, in return, found herself lighter. Smiling more. Living again instead of simply existing.

Even her coworkers noticed. "You've been glowing lately," one of them said. "Who's the reason?"
Jaida only smiled. "Just me, finally breathing."

But deep down, she knew better.

That night she laid across her bed, half watching TV, half listening to her dad on speakerphone. His laugh filled the room like music from a memory.

"You sound chipper tonight," he teased. "What's got my girl cheesing through the phone like that? Don't tell me you found somebody who can make you laugh harder than your old man."

Jaida chuckled. "Maybe I did. His name's Jackson."

"Ah, I knew it! There's a man behind that smile." He paused. "What's he do?"

"He works for the Melanie Lenora Foundation," she said.

"The what now?" he asked with a confused tone.

Before she could answer, her mom's voice cut in from somewhere nearby.

"Melanie Lenora Foundation? Oh, I've heard of them! They focus on helping families of people with terminal illness, right? Jaida, is that the same one that—"

"Woman," her dad interrupted, laughing, "let the girl breathe. That's not why she called."

Her mom huffed. "I'm just asking questions!"

Jaida laughed. "It's okay, Mom. I'll tell you more later. Promise."

"We're just happy to hear that happiness in your voice again," her dad said warmly. "Been a minute since we've heard that."

"Yeah," Jaida murmured. "It feels good."

"So, you ready for tomorrow?" he asked. "Don't think you're getting out of this hike. We're starting early."

"I'm ready," she said. "It's Mom we have to convince."

"Excuse me?" her mom called. "I *can* hike. I just don't *enjoy* pretending I'm being chased by wild animals for fitness."

Her dad burst out laughing. "You just don't like sweating. That's your problem."

"I like clean cardio — mall walking and grocery store sprints," she fired back.

"That's my lady," her dad said, still laughing. "Complaining the whole time but she'll show up anyway."

"Only because I love you two," she said.

"And we love you right back," her dad replied, voice full of that easy affection that always made her smile.

They stayed on the phone a little longer, the conversation drifting from small jokes to weekend plans and which snacks her mom insisted on packing for the hike. By the time they hung up, Jaida was still smiling — the kind of quiet smile that lingered long after the call ended.

She glanced toward the window, the night sky stretching endless and calm, and thought about how good it felt to have something to look forward to again.

Her phone buzzed, and she glanced down to see a new text.

> **Jackson:** I want to see you tonight. Just us. Can you?

Her pulse quickened. The idea of seeing him made the world feel lighter, somehow brighter.

> **Jaida:** Yes… I can.

She typed back, her fingers trembling slightly.

Jackson smiled, though his thoughts were entirely on her. He thought of her laugh, the spark in her eyes, the small moments of vulnerability she'd shown him, and the way he wanted tonight to be about her—just her.

The city lulled by the time Jackson parked his car by the lake. Streetlights shimmered across the water, casting gold and silver reflections on the dark surface. The only sounds were the occasional rustle of leaves and the distant call of a bird. He killed the engine, leaving the soft swish of the lake to fill the quiet between them.

Jaida slid lower into the passenger seat, tugging her jacket tighter around herself. The car felt private, a small world removed from everything else. She glanced at him. Curiosity mingled with nervous anticipation.

"So… tell me", she began, voice low, hesitant. "Why are you single, Jackson? With everything you do, everything about you… why hasn't someone made an honest man out of you yet?"

Jackson let out a quiet, almost rueful laugh. He stared at the lake, measuring the reflection of the stars before speaking. "I was… betrayed once," he said finally, voice low and deliberate. "By someone I trusted completely. It was… unforgivable. I haven't shared it with anyone—because it's not something I can easily forget. And after that… I've been careful. Very careful."

Jaida nodded, feeling the heaviness tucked between his words. She knew he wasn't ready to go deeper, so she didn't press. His eyes held a quiet truth, and for a moment, the world beyond the car faded, leaving only the two of them suspended in that fragile, honest space.

After a quiet beat, he turned toward her, his voice soft with genuine interest. "What about you? You come off strong, but… I can tell you've lived through things you don't share with just anyone. What made you who you are, Jaida?"

She drew in a slow breath; her eyes fixed on the dark water ahead. "Honestly… I've been through a lot," she said, her voice steady but brushed with a delicate crack of truth. "And after everything, being single just… felt safer."

Jackson turned a little in his seat, one arm draping along the back of hers. "Tell me, "He said softly, not pressing, not demanding—just inviting. "What does 'a lot' mean for you?"

Jaida kept her gaze on the water at first. The moonlight slid across its surface like a long silver ribbon, and she followed it with her eyes as if it might help her find the right words. Her fingers picked at the seam of her leggings, slow and restless. The truth caught in her throat—not because she didn't trust him, but because saying it out loud felt like peeling back a layer she'd worked hard to stitch closed.

She exhaled, long and shaky.

"There were relationships that took more from me than they ever gave," she began, her voice barely above the whisper of the waves. "People who claimed they loved me but only loved the comfort I provided. People who saw my strength as something to lean on... or something to dim."

Jackson's expression softened. He didn't interrupt. Didn't shift in a way that told her to hurry. Just listened—fully, intently, the way someone listens when it matters.

She swallowed, staring at her own reflection in the window now—her face faint, ghostlike against the backdrop of the lake. "And when you get tired of breaking and healing and breaking again... you start thinking maybe silence is safer. Maybe solitude means fewer disappointments. Maybe it's better to hold yourself than to hand your heart to someone who won't treat it right."

The wind brushed through her curls as if trying to soothe her, and she tucked a stray strand behind her ear.

"I got used to being the one people leaned on," she continued, her voice steadier now, "but I didn't have anyone I could lean on. Not really. Not consistently. Being single wasn't about not wanting love. It was about protecting my peace."

Jackson let her words settle. The gravity of them filled the small space of the car, warm and heavy.

He shifted just enough to face her fully, his eyes searching hers through the dimness.

"I get that," he said quietly. "More than you think."

His thumb brushed the edge of her knuckles—not holding, not grabbing, just a gentle, grounding touch that felt like an unspoken promise.

"But Jaida..." His voice dipped, low and sincere. "What if you didn't have to do everything alone anymore? What if safety didn't have to equal solitude?"

Her fingers flexed lightly against the leather armrest, heart beginning to race at the question. She swallowed, taking a slow, deliberate breath to steady herself. "There's... a lot you don't know," she admitted, "and I don't even know where to start". Her eyes drifted to the shimmering water outside and she paused before saying "I was raped when I was sixteen."

Jackson's hand hovered near hers. His chest tightened at her words. "I'm so sorry," he murmured softly. "No one should ever have to go through that."

She swallowed again, trying to stay steady, and the memory came alive in her mind:

"The basement... damp air, hum of a deep freezer, dim yellow light. The ceiling paint was chipped, and I counted the chips over and over, just to feel like I could control something."

Her shoulders rose subtly, hands pressing into the armrest as the memory tightened around her. Her jaw trembled slightly.

Jackson's body responded instinctively. Anger flared inside him at the thought of anyone hurting her, sharp and hot. He clenched his fists briefly but forced himself to breathe, to contain it. He couldn't let her see the rage; he didn't want her to shut down, to retreat behind the walls she had built so carefully. He wanted her to feel safe. Protected. Seen.

Gently, he reached out, letting the back of his hand brush against hers. Just a light touch at first, a lifeline without forcing it. She didn't pull away. Instead, he let his fingers rest over hers, a quiet reassurance that he was there.

Tears slipped down her cheeks. Without a word, Jackson lifted his hand and brushed them away, careful and tender. His voice was low, steady, deliberate: "Breathe with me. In… out. You're safe, Jaida. I've got you."

She let out a shaky exhale, her body still trembling from the echo of trauma, but the presence of his steady hand and unwavering gaze drew her back into the present. Her anxiety ebbed slightly under his calm energy, her nervous system responding to the rare, calming reassurance he radiated.

"Good," he murmured. "Just let it go. You don't have to carry that right now. Not here. Not with me."

A few more tears fell. He kept his touch gentle but present, his eyes never leaving hers. "It's okay. You're here. You're safe. I'm right here."

She finally allowed herself to exhale fully, shoulders easing slightly, pulse slowing. The lake outside shimmered in the distance, quiet and constant.

This… this is rare, she realized, letting the smallest thread of trust extend outward from years of guarded walls. Few people had ever made her feel safe enough to lower them.

Her voice trembled, but she pressed on, revealing pieces of her past she had never spoken aloud. "Then… Luther," she whispered, her hands turned into fists pressing into the armrest. "He was… violent. He left bruises in places no one would ever see. And one day, I was at the mall with my best friend, Brandon, when he came up to us. He started mocking me… joking about how he'd made me do things I didn't want to do. Brandon saw the way I shrank, the way I froze, and he didn't hesitate—he confronted him right there, made sure he knew not to touch me again. Monday… she helped me get Brandon's bail."

Jackson's chest tightened again, the protective fire flaring, and he clenched his jaw, forcing himself to focus on composing her instead of lashing out. "I'm glad your friend stood up for you," he said gently, voice rough with emotion. "Someone had to fight when you couldn't."

Jaida nodded, a fragile, sad smile tugging at her lips. "Yeah… that's what he said too. Only Monday and him know. No one else."

Jackson exhaled slowly. "I understand. And you're strong. Strong for surviving. Strong for carrying it and still showing up in the world."

She looked at him, eyes glistening in the soft glow of the dashboard lights, and whispered, "Thanks."

They sat in silence, the gentle wash of waves and distant calls of birds wrapping them in quiet understanding. Jackson kept his presence steady, protective, patient—letting her process at her own pace, letting her feel safe without judgment or rush. Every small tremor, every sigh, every drop of tears only strengthened his resolve: to protect her, to hold the space for her, to be someone she could trust utterly.

And for Jaida, each slow breath with him, each touch, each calm word was a small miracle—a rare, precious sense of safety she had almost forgotten existed.

After a long moment, Jaida's voice softened, almost a whisper. "That's… most of it. The pieces I've never shared. I didn't want anyone to see that side of me."

Jackson gave a slow, reassuring nod, his thumb brushing against the back of her hand in a steady rhythm. "You don't have to hide it with me," he said softly. "I'm not going anywhere. And I don't just want to hear the pain—I want to know all of you. The brave, the strong, the real you."

Her lips pressed together in a small, tentative smile. "It's... hard to let anyone see that."

"I know," he muttered softly, eyes never leaving hers. "And I won't rush you. You set the pace. I'll follow."

For a few minutes, they sat in silence, listening to the gentle lap of the lake against the shore, the soft pulse of the city muted behind them. The air felt cooler now, softer, carrying the faint scent of water and night air. Jackson shifted slightly, his shoulder brushing hers in a subtle way. It was a quiet intimacy, one that spoke louder than words.

Jaida finally exhaled fully, letting some of the tension in her body dissolve. "I don't... I don't know how to explain it," she said, voice small. "It feels... lighter, somehow, just having someone listen. Someone... not afraid."

Jackson's chest warmed at her words. "I'm glad," he said, voice low and earnest. "I want to be that person for you. Not just tonight, but... whenever you need me."

A small laugh escaped her lips, a sound she hadn't realized she'd been holding back. "You're... persistent," she teased softly, glancing at him with a faint spark in her eyes.

"I have my ways," he said with a soft, playful smile, letting just a hint of the tension lift from the car.

The corner of the lake glimmered under the reflection of the moonlight, and for the first time that evening, Jaida let herself lean just slightly into his presence. Not physically, not entirely—but emotionally. The walls she had built so carefully weren't gone, they couldn't be—but the thread of trust that had formed tonight felt real, and strong.

Jackson noticed the small shift in her, the easing of her shoulders, the softening of her gaze. He reached over, gently brushing a stray strand of hair behind her ear. "You're safe," he confessed, just above a whisper. "And you're not alone."

Her eyes glistened again, but this time there were no fresh tears, only the quiet acknowledgment of comfort she rarely allowed herself to feel. She nodded faintly, offering him a fragile, but genuine, smile.

They stayed there for a while longer, talking quietly about small, ordinary things, favorite books, the city skyline, the peacefulness of the lake at night.

The conversation was gentle, a tender counterpoint to the heaviness of what she had shared. And in the soft glow of the dashboard lights, in the stillness of the night, the bond between them deepened—built on trust, care, and the rare, fragile comfort of being truly seen.

The ride back from the lake was quiet, the city lights blurred past the windows, a soft glow in the dark. Jaida sat beside him, her body more relaxed than when she had arrived, though traces of tension still lingered in the subtle rise and fall of her shoulders. Neither spoke much; words had already done their work tonight, carving a fragile bridge of trust between them.

When he finally pulled up in front of her townhome, Jackson put the car in park. The soft purr of the engine seemed louder in the stillness of the night. He turned to look at her, catching the faint reflection of the dashboard lights in her eyes.

"You don't have to say anything more tonight," he said softly. "Just... remember that you're not alone."

She gave a small and tired smile. "Thank you... for everything tonight. For listening. For... this."

He nodded, voice low and steady. "Always."

After a pause, he asked lightly, "So... what do you have planned for tomorrow?"

Jaida glanced back at him with a soft grin, grateful he shifted the conversation and cut through the awkward tension she'd been feeling. "My parents want to go on a hike. Thought I'd join them—get some fresh air, a little exercise."

Jackson's face stayed composed, but his smile warmed, lingering a beat too long. "That sounds like a good day... and a solid workout," he said softly. His eyes held hers for a moment, full of quiet encouragement. "You should get some rest so you're ready for it."

She nodded gently. "Yeah... I should probably go in."

"Yeah," he echoed, his voice soft. "Sleep well."

They exchanged quiet goodnights, the kind that felt warmer than the word itself. She reached for the door handle, and for a moment, neither of them moved. Jackson stayed still in his seat, watching her in the soft glow of the dashboard lights, wishing he could keep her there just a little longer.

He wanted to pull her into his arms, to hold her until the world felt simple again—but after everything she'd shared with him, he wouldn't risk crossing a boundary she hadn't invited him past. So, he let the moment stay gentle, unpressured.

When she finally slipped out of the car and closed the door, Jackson let out a slow, quiet exhale. The calm in his voice belying the ache in his chest. He wanted to see her again tomorrow, to hold her close after giving her space tonight, to let the world shrink down to just the two of them for a little while. Instead, he let the words he'd said hang between them, steady and quiet, while the longing he couldn't voice twisted softly inside him.

He sat in the car for a long moment, staring at the street in front of him. His hands rested lightly on the steering wheel, but his mind was elsewhere. Every word she had revealed, every pause, every tremor in her voice, every glimmer of strength—it all replayed in vivid detail.

The basement. Luther. Brandon. Monday. Every part of her story—the fear, the pain, the resilience—settled into him like a weight he couldn't ignore. And the more he thought about it, the more his chest tightened in a way that had nothing to do with anger or protectiveness.

He realized he felt something he hadn't expected. Something deeper than concern, stronger than empathy. A pull toward her that was more than wanting to protect her, more than wanting to comfort her—it was personal, visceral, undeniable.

Yet even as he sat there, letting the vibration of the city seep through the car's windows, he didn't allow himself to name it. Not yet. He only knew he cared, profoundly and irrevocably, in a way that unsettled him and thrilled him all at once.

With another slow exhale, he finally drove off into the night, the reflection of the lake still shimmering in his mind, and the sound of her voice echoing softly in his chest.

He didn't know where this would go. He only knew that after tonight, he couldn't ignore the way she made him feel—and that feeling was already strong enough to change everything.

Jaida unlocked her front door and stepped inside, shedding her jacket and shoes with a quiet sigh. The night was still lingering in her mind—the soft lap of the lake, the shimmer of the moon across the water, the warmth of his hand brushing hers, the steady rhythm of his voice grounding her when the memories had threatened to overwhelm.

She sank onto the edge of her bed, letting herself exhale fully for the first time in hours. *No has ever calmed me like that. Not even close.* Her fingers traced the comforter beneath her, feeling the familiar textures, easing herself in the ordinary after the intensity of the evening.

The memory of his steady presence, the gentle reassurance, the patience he'd shown—it was rare, almost dizzying in its effect. Her pulse, still lingering from the echo of trauma and anxiety, finally slowed.

She felt safe. Truly safe. And it wasn't just physical safety; it was the feeling of being seen, of being understood without judgement, of being allowed to exist without the burden of fear pressing down on her chest.

A small, tentative smile tugged at her lips as she thought about him. She realized, in a quiet way that made her chest flutter, that she liked him in a way that went beyond gratitude, beyond comfort. He had touched parts of her that were usually guarded, parts that very few people had ever glimpsed.

I like him. I really do. He's different.

There was no grand declaration in her chest, no surge of certainty. Just the steady, undeniable pull she felt toward him. The relief. The safety. The warmth. The way her thoughts kept circling back to him, as if her mind refused to let go of the night, of him, of how completely he had held space for her.

She leaned back against the headboard, closing her eyes and letting the memories wash over her. The laughter they had shared, the silences that felt comfortable, the quiet moments of trust—it all lingered like a soft echo in her chest.

And for the first time in a long time, Jaida allowed herself to hope. Hope that maybe, just maybe, there could be more nights like this. More moments where someone saw her, truly saw her, and let her be safe without judgment.

That alone made her heart feel lighter than it had in years. She smiled, imagining resting in his arms, feeling the quiet safety only he seemed to offer. *I can't wait to see him again*, she added silently, a small flutter of excitement—and a deeper ache of longing—warming her chest.

The next morning dawned crisp and golden. Sunlight spilled across the park, catching on blades of dew so they sparkled like tiny jewels. The air smelled faintly of wet grass and earth, fresh and clean.

By the car, her dad was already moving through an exaggerated set of stretches, bending and twisting with theatrical flair, his laughter carrying through the quiet morning.

"You sure you don't need a warm-up, old man?" Jaida teased.

"Please," he said, straightening with a pop of his back. "I still got it."

Her mom rolled her eyes. "He's been saying that since '98."

"And I've been proving it ever since," he shot back with a grin, adjusting the strap of his backpack. "Come on, woman, let's move before I lose momentum."

"You lost that years ago," she teased, falling into step beside him.

Jaida laughed, shaking her head as she zipped up her jacket. The morning air was cool enough to sting her cheeks, but it felt good — crisp, alive. The kind of weather that made everything smell clean and new.

They started down the wooded trail — Jaida between them, the sound of crunching leaves beneath their shoes. The air smelled of pine and damp earth. Her dad cracked jokes the entire way, laughing before anyone else did. Her mom sighed and smiled, pretending to lag behind just to get him talking.

The trail gradually opened, and a gentle breeze carried the earthy scent of the lake up to them. Jaida could see the water shimmering through the trees, silver and still, mist hovering like a delicate veil over the surface.

Her dad paused mid-step, hands on his hips, taking in the view as if he'd never seen it before. "See? Worth it," he said, voice full of pride and satisfaction. "Look at that."

Her mom stopped a few feet behind, arms crossed, pretending to frown at the incline but secretly scanning the lake with a soft smile. "My calves disagree," she muttered, though the corners of her mouth twitched upward.

Jaida slowed, letting the quiet wash over her for a moment. The leaves beneath her shoes crunched in soft harmony with distant birdsong. Sunlight flickered through the canopy, dappling her jacket in patches of gold.

Her dad lifted his arms toward the sky like he was claiming the moment for himself. "Worth every single step," he said, looking at them both with that mischievous glint in his eyes.

Her mom brushed her hand through her hair and glanced around. "You know," she said, "we could make this perfect — set up a little picnic. Just grab some blankets, maybe sandwiches, some juice..."

Her dad groaned dramatically. "Woman, you pack enough snacks for a small army every time we go anywhere!"

"Exactly," she said, wagging a finger playfully. "We're *already* here, we might as well enjoy it properly."

Jaida laughed, imagining her mom laying out a blanket in the middle of the woods with her carefully labeled Tupperware. The idea was absurd but somehow fitting.

Jaida took a step closer to them, feeling the warmth of their presence, the ease of their laughter mingling with the light breeze. Her mom, ever the dramatist, placed a hand on her hip and shook her head. "You two are impossible," she said, though her tone lacked bite.

Her dad swung an arm around her mom's shoulders. "Woman, admit it — you're glad you came."

"I'm glad for the company," she said softly, leaning into him.

Jaida took a deep breath, letting the crisp air fill her lungs. She watched her parents—their little quirks, their easy teasing, the warmth in their smiles—and felt a quiet, almost sacred sense of gratitude.

And as her thoughts drifted to Jackson, she realized she felt the same calm certainty he brought into her life, the quiet steadiness that made ordinary moments feel lighter, somehow fuller.

With these connections—her parents and Jackson—the world seemed full, peaceful, and right—for now.

Chapter Seven

The Coldest Room

The day unraveled like a thread pulled too fast—snapping, fraying, impossible to gather back together.

It began with the sound of laughter. Her father had been walking a few paces ahead, smiling as he brushed a bug from his arm, his easy warmth filling the air like it always did when they were outside together. Jaida remembered thinking how good it felt—being in nature with him, away from all the noise, just breathing fresh air.

Then it happened.

One moment, he was reaching for his water bottle. The next, he jerked suddenly, swatting at his neck as he brushed away a bee. But his hand didn't fall back to his side, it clawed at his throat, fingers digging in as though trying to pry open an invisible grip. His chest heaved for air that wouldn't come. His face flushed red, then darkened toward a frightening purple, his lips swelling, his breaths breaking into sharp, ragged gasps.

"Dad!" Jaida cried, rushing forward. She had seen anaphylaxis before, in textbooks, even once in clinicals—but never here, never with her own father. Her nurse's brain screamed instructions: *Epinephrine. Airway. Oxygen. Call for help.* But they were out in the woods, miles from the nearest road.

Her mother's hands fumbled with her phone, trembling so hard she almost dropped it. "Please, please, hurry," she begged into the receiver, her voice breaking as she gave their location.

Jaida pressed her hand against his chest, counting each shallow, failing breath. "Stay with us, Dad. Just stay with us." Her own voice sounded foreign, high-pitched and frantic, nothing like the calm she had been trained to hold.

By the time the ambulance tore down the gravel road, sirens slicing the quiet, Jaida already knew.

The paramedics rushed to work, voices clipped, movements fast, but she could read the flatness in their faces, the lack of response in her father's body. She knew the odds, knew what it meant when every second stretched without change. But she couldn't say it out loud. Not with her mother's tear-streaked eyes locked on hers, desperate for hope.

So, Jaida plastered hope on her face like a mask and kept whispering, "They've got him, Mom. We're going to be okay." Every word felt like a lie clawing its way out of her throat. The nurse in her knew the brutal truth—she wasn't supposed to promise anything. They were trained never to tell people their loved one would be okay in the hospital. And yet, seeing her mom's trembling hands and desperate eyes, Jaida couldn't bring herself to shatter her hope. Even if it meant swallowing the truth herself.

At the hospital, fluorescent lights buzzed overhead as the staff whisked him behind closed doors.

Minutes blurred, then stretched, then tangled into something unbearable. They kept taking turns walking up to the front desk—first her mother, voice tight with worry, then Jaida, trying to keep hers even. Every time, the answer was the same:

"He's not in the system yet."
"Someone will be with you soon."
"We'll let you know as soon as we have anything."

Her mother paced the tiled floor in an agitated loop, arms folded, unfolding, folded again—like she was trying to hold herself together and failing. The soft squeak of her shoes, the buzz of fluorescent lights, the distant beeps deeper in the ER—they all grated against the tension already coiled sharp inside her.

Jaida stayed still, anchored to her chair, posture composed in a way that almost looked calm. But inside, her mind was bracing—quietly, methodically—preparing for the worst even as she whispered to herself not yet, not yet, not yet.

She watched the doors every time they hissed open. She held her breath every time a nurse walked by.

And then, finally, a nurse approached. Her expression was gentle, but her eyes told Jaida everything she'd been trying not to imagine.

"Can you come with me?" she asked softly.

They followed the nurse down a long corridor, passing bustling stations where nurses called out orders and monitors chirped in uneven rhythms. The sharper scents of antiseptic and something metallic clung to the air. Every step felt heavier than the last.

The nurse stopped at a door tucked into the far corner of the hall. When she opened it, the quiet inside felt unnatural—too still, too intentional. The room was small, almost claustrophobic. White walls without a single scuff or picture. No windows. Just four chairs arranged around a narrow table that suddenly felt too flimsy to carry what was coming.

The cold struck Jaida immediately—not a draft, not the sterile chill of hospital air conditioning, but something deeper. A cold that seeped slowly into her arms and down her spine, settling beneath her skin. If the morgue was the coldest place in the building, this room couldn't have been far behind.

The door clicked softly a moment later. A doctor stepped in, his expression somber, shoulders slightly slumped as though he already carried the weight of their grief. His eyes met theirs, and in that single glance, Jaida felt the air in her lungs go thin.

"We did everything we could," he said quietly. "I'm so sorry. He didn't make it."

Her mother's cry broke open the silence like glass shattering—raw, keening, uncontainable. She doubled over as if the words had physically struck her, sinking into the nearest chair. Her hands covered her face, rocking with each sob as fractured whispers tumbled out:

"What if I... what if I could have done something? What if I had—"

Jaida dropped to her knees beside her mother, the cold linoleum pressing through her leggings as she wrapped both hands around her mother's trembling ones. She held them tightly—steady, secure—because her mother felt like she might fall apart in her palms.

"Mom," she said, her voice low but firm, fighting to stay steady. "Stop. You called 911. You did everything right. There was nothing else. Nothing."

The words scraped out of her like they had edges. Each one tasted bitter, because even as she said them, a part of her— the part trained to scan for symptoms, solutions, missed signs—kept whispering its own cruel thoughts.

If only she'd had epinephrine.
If only she could have opened the airway in time.
If only they'd been closer, faster, luckier.

Each thought clawed at her, threatening to take hold. But she forced them back, burying them beneath a layer of discipline she'd had to learn the hard way. She couldn't afford to break now. Not with her mother unraveling beside her.

She squeezed her mother's hands again, grounding herself in the warmth, in the reality of the moment, in the responsibility of it.

She had to be strong—for Mom.

And for herself.

Because even now, beneath the faint buzz of hospital lights and her mother's shaking breaths, Jaida could feel it—the shift. The tightening.

The doctor didn't say much as he guided Jaida and her mother down the hallway—just a quiet "This way," spoken with the heaviness of someone who had done this too many times.

The closer they got to the room, the more the world seemed to narrow. The overhead lights buzzed faintly, the smell of antiseptic thickened, and every footstep echoed like it was happening in the wrong place, in the wrong version of reality.

When they stepped inside, Jaida's breath caught.

Her father lay on a stretcher in the center of the small ED room, the sheets tucked neatly around him. His face looked peaceful, as though he were only sleeping—resting after a long day.

If it weren't for the stillness, if it weren't for the absence of the rise and fall of his chest, she could have believed this was all a mistake.

This couldn't be real.
This couldn't be him.

Her hands trembled as she stepped closer. She reached for his wrist—the skin cool beneath her fingers—and turned it gently until the hospital band came into view. She stared at the name printed in block letters.

It was him.
There was no waking up from this.

Beside her, her mother quietly dragged a chair to the head of the stretcher. The metal legs scraped softly against the floor. She sank into it without a word, her eyes locked on her husband's face, her expression hollowed out by shock. She didn't cry, didn't speak—she just stared, as if memorizing every inch of him before he slipped away for good.

A few minutes later, the door opened again. A nurse stepped inside, guiding several members of her father's family into the room. They entered in a tight cluster, whispers dying on their lips as they saw the body.

They stayed near the corner, refusing to come any closer. Their faces were drawn, stiff, unreadable at first—until their eyes shifted toward her mother.

Then the daggers came.

Sharp, silent, unmistakable.

Jaida felt their judgment settle over the room like smoke. She didn't need to hear their words to know exactly what they were thinking.

How could you let this happen?
Why weren't you paying attention?
Why weren't you watching him?

She straightened her spine, jaw tightening. If she showed even an inch of vulnerability, they would sink their teeth in. She had learned that years ago—his family had never been kind to her mother. But grief sharpened their dislike into something colder, something meaner.

And this was only the beginning.

Because in the days that followed, their cruelty would deepen.

It always did.

The hospital's fluorescent lights buzzed overhead as Jaida and her mother walked through the corridor side by side— two shadows moving through a world that suddenly felt too bright, too sharp, too loud.

The automatic doors whooshed open ahead of them, letting in a blast of cold night air. It smelled like rain on pavement, like metal, like the kind of quiet that follows disaster.

Behind them, her father's family lingered in the waiting area, their whispers still snaking through the hall. But Jaida and her mother didn't look back. Not for a second.

They had made it through the viewing without breaking. They had swallowed their grief like stones, burying every tremble, every sob that wanted to claw its way out. In front of his family, they were steel. They were control. They were dignity poured into human form.

Now, as they stepped into the parking lot, the night felt vast and empty, the only sound the echo of their footsteps on the concrete.

Her mother's hands were shaking so hard she tucked them into her pockets. Jaida pretended not to notice. She knew pretending was its own kind of mercy.

They reached their cars—parked only two spaces apart—and paused, both leaning against the cold metal as if it were the only solid thing left.

"You good to drive?" Jaida asked softly, though her own legs felt like water.

Her mother nodded, too quickly. "I'll... manage."

There was nothing to say. No words strong enough to hold up the moment. No conversation that could patch the hole carved into both of them.

So, they stood there for a beat—just breathing, just existing—before her mother straightened, lifting her chin with that quiet resilience she'd shown all night.

"We'll get through this together," she whispered, her voice thin but steady.

Jaida nodded, her throat tightening. "Always."

They opened their car doors at the same time, the dull thud of metal closing sounding final in a way neither of them wanted to acknowledge.

The drive home blurred. Streetlights streaked across Jaida's windshield like smears of gold, but she barely registered any of it. Her hands stayed locked at ten and two, numb and rigid, steering out of habit more than intention. Her mind was fog, thick and disorienting, like she was moving through water.

How am I even doing this?
How is she?

It was like autopilot had grabbed the wheel. Grief had emptied them out so completely that only instinct remained—turn here, brake there, keep going.

When Jaida finally pulled into her driveway, she didn't get out right away. She sat still, keys in her trembling hand, her chest tight from holding everything in.

Jaida stared at her phone for a long moment, the screen glowing against the dim light of the cabin. Her hands were trembling—so much so that she had to steady her wrist against her knee just to type.

The world around her felt muffled, like someone had wrapped everything in thick cotton: the air, the sounds, even her thoughts.

She typed the words, erased them, typed them again. Nothing felt right. Nothing felt real. After a hollow exhale, she finally settled on the only sentence she could manage.

> **Jaida:** My dad died.

No explanation. No details. Just the truth she couldn't carry alone anymore.

Her thumb hovered for half a second, then she hit send. The message left her phone with a soft whoosh—too gentle for something so devastating. Immediately, her breath stuttered. Her stomach flipped. Her heart thumped painfully against her ribs.

She set the phone in the cup holder beside her, and wrapped her arms around herself, rocking slightly, as if motion alone could soften the ache tearing through her chest.

The reply came faster than she expected.

> **Jackson:** I'm so sorry, Jaida. You don't have to explain. Just tell me

what you need. Don't try to carry
this by yourself.

Jaida pressed her forehead against the steering wheel, eyes burning, breath hitching.

The compassion in his words cracked something in her and for the first time that night, she let a single tear fall—quiet, hidden, safe in the privacy of her unmoving car.

Her phone buzzed.

Mom: Home.

Jaida's fingers moved mechanically as she typed back.

Jaida: Home too.

Another message came.
Short. Simple. Breaking.

Mom: I love you.

She typed back through the blur.

Jaida: I love you too.

Tears spilled over, hot and unrestrained, dripping onto her phone screen. She didn't even bother wiping them away. She just let herself cry, shoulders shaking, breath breaking— before gathering herself, stepping out into the cool night air, and forcing her legs to carry her inside.

Stronger together. Even when separated by two different houses, two different cars, and a grief too heavy for words.

As Jaida was sitting on the edge of her bed, still in the clothes she'd worn to on the hike, her phone lit up.

Monday calling.

For a moment, she considered letting it ring. Her chest still felt bruised from crying, her eyes gritty and swollen. But Monday didn't call unless it mattered. So, she swiped to answer.

"Hey, babe," Monday said softly—so gently Jaida nearly broke all over again. "I... I heard about what happened with your dad. Are you okay?"

Jaida swallowed, her voice barely steady. "I'm... holding on."

"And your mom? How's she doing?" Monday asked, already bracing for the answer.

"She's... trying," Jaida said. "It's hitting her every hour in a new way."

There was a pause, not empty—just full. Full of care. Full of someone who'd known her long enough to hear everything she wasn't saying.

Then Monday sighed, long and annoyed, her tone shifting. "And girl, I heard about his family. Lord. I hope they can act like they got some sense for once. But knowing them..." She clicked her tongue. "I doubt it."

A tired laugh pushed out of Jaida. "Yeah... I don't have much faith, either. My dad was always the one keeping everybody in line. He was the mediator. And now that he's gone?" She shook her head. "All bets are off."

"Oh, absolutely," Monday said. "Remember that one time—" she broke into a laugh before she could even finish—"when your aunt tried to start that drama at the cookout? Talking slick like she forgot where she was?"

Jaida smiled, the memory sliding in warm. "Oh my, yes. And my dad walked right up behind her like, 'Ma'am... please don't make me embarrass you in front of your plate.'"

Both of them burst into laughter. Monday kept going.

"And she tried to argue—tried! But he hit her with that 'I'm only going to say this once' tone." Monday laughed harder. "And she sat her behind DOWN. Quiet as a church mouse."

Jaida wiped a tear, but this one wasn't from grief. "He always knew how to shut down the foolishness."

"Oh, he was the king of shutting stuff down," Monday agreed. "Remember when the four of us went to Cedar Point? And your mom was screaming on that roller coaster, and your dad was laughing the whole time like it was Saturday night at the comedy club?"

Jaida's smile softened. "He held my hand the whole climb up the first hill. Said he wasn't letting me fly out the seat."

"And then afterward we all ate those giant turkey legs and pretended those unseasoned things were good," Monday said, snorting. "We were so dramatic."

The warmth in the memory hit Jaida in the center of her chest—soft, sweet, painful in that beautiful way grief sometimes is.

Monday's voice gentled again. "Jaida... I'm really sorry you're going through this. I can't imagine how heavy everything feels right now."

Jaida felt her throat tighten. "Yeah... it's a lot."

"I know," Monday whispered. "And listen... I'm here. For you, and for your mom. Whatever you need. You don't even have to ask—just call. Or text. Or send smoke signals. I'll show up."

Jaida's voice cracked when she answered. "Thank you, Monday."

"I mean it, babe. I got you. Both of you." Monday exhaled softly, giving her space. "Get some rest, okay? Just... try."

"Yeah," Jaida murmured. "I will."

They hung up, and the room fell quiet again—but not as heavy. Not as dark.

Monday had given her something she didn't even realize she needed:

A reminder of love.

A reminder of laughter.

A reminder of who her father had been.

And that she wasn't going through any of this alone.

Chapter Eight

Where Love Stood Still

The house Jaida grew up in felt hollow all morning. Every corner echoing with absence—until the first knock sounded. Then another. And another.

Friends of Jaida's parents arrived carrying foil-covered dishes, bags of groceries, warm embraces. Her mother's siblings trickled in next, followed by Monday with her usual soft, calming presence.

Soon, the dining table was covered in casseroles, homemade pound cake, rotisserie chickens, fruit trays—love disguised as food.

Conversation slowly wove through the quiet. They gathered in the living room, flipping through old photo albums, spreading loose pictures across the coffee table. Every image held a story, a memory, a moment they weren't sure they were ready to relive. But they did it together laughing at the old hairstyles, sighing at the tender memories, wiping away the tears that slipped out despite their efforts to keep steady.

The house didn't feel empty anymore. For the first time since the hospital, warmth seeped back into the walls.

Jaida arrived a little later, stepping into an atmosphere alive with crosstalk and soft laughter. Everyone greeted her with hugs and gentle looks. She hugged her mother, squeezed Monday's hand, then sat beside her mom to help pick photos for the obituary.

It was painstaking, every picture felt heavy, sacred. Anyone watching could see Jaida's throat tightening each time her hand lingered on her father's face frozen in a moment of joy.

Her phone rang. **Jackson.**

"Hello", she answered quietly while stepping into the hallway.

"Where are you?" he asked, his voice steady and warm.

"At my parents' house. Everyone's here helping."

"Send me the address."

She didn't think twice. They hung up, she sent the address and tucked the phone away before rejoining the group.

About thirty minutes later, a soft knock sounded again. Monday peeked through the window, and her eyebrows rose with a grin spreading across her face.

Jackson stepped inside holding a bottle of Jaida's favorite wine. Monday's mom—Milan—followed his entrance with amused, knowing eyes.

"Who is *that*?" Milan whispered, leaning closer to Monday.

Monday smiled. "Her knight in shining armor."

Jaida looked up and her breath caught for a moment before she stood to greet him. Jackson offered the wine to her mother with genuine warmth.

"I'm so sorry for your loss," he said gently.

Her mom accepted it with a grateful nod. "Thank you so much."

Milan motioned toward the kitchen. "We have plenty of food—come make a plate."

Jackson agreed, and he and Jaida slipped into the kitchen. She fixed a plate for him, arranging everything just right. Her mother stepped in briefly to place his wine on ice, giving them a small, soft smile before returning to the living room.

Soon, Jackson sat at the dining table with everyone, eating, listening, contributing where he could, letting Jaida's family pull him into their stories. He fit seamlessly into the moment, offering presence without taking space.

Meanwhile, Milan tugged Jaida gently by the elbow and led her into a quieter corner of the hallway.

"So," Milan said, folding her arms, eyes sharp with playful suspicion. "Who is this, Jackson?"

Jaida exhaled, a little flustered. "Just a friend."

Milan raised an eyebrow so high it practically touched her hairline. "Oh, I don't believe that for one second."

"Auntie—"

"No, no," Milan cut in, wagging a finger lightly. "A man who shows up the way *he* just did? With wine, with presence, with intention? Baby, that's not 'just a friend.' None of your other friends are here doing what he's doing."

Jaida looked down at her hands, heat rising in her cheeks despite everything going on.

Milan softened, placing a hand on her shoulder. "I'm not saying you have to be ready for anything right now. But I *am* saying—men like him don't fall out of the sky every day."

Jaida glanced toward the dining room where Jackson sat listening to one of her uncles tell an old story, leaning in with genuine interest. Her heart pulled in a way she wasn't ready to name.

Jackson sat at the dining room table with a plate of food he barely tasted, listening politely as Jaida's family drifted through stories—some funny, some bittersweet, some that made the whole room grow quiet for a beat. But no matter who was talking or how loud the room became, his attention kept drifting back to Jaida.

Across the room, she was bent over an open photo album with Monday, her shoulder brushing her cousin's as they whispered about which pictures to choose. Every so often, she'd smile—small, soft, almost hesitant, like her face wasn't used to forming that shape right now. But when that smile did come, even briefly, something tugged at him so sharply it almost made him inhale.

God... she is beautiful, he thought. *Not fragile—though she was hurting. Not broken—though she was grieving. Just... pure. Honest. Real in a way that most people didn't know how to be.*

He watched her tuck a strand of hair behind her ear, watched the way she held a picture of her father gently, like it was a living thing. He saw the flicker of pain in her eyes she tried so hard to hide. And he saw—clear as day—the strength right underneath it.

Her family had welcomed him with warmth he hadn't expected. They joked with him, fed him, pulled him into memories like he'd been there. But even with all the chatter, he kept tracing Jaida's presence like a gravitational pull he didn't quite understand.

She looked up at him once, across the room. Just a brief glance. But her eyes softened when they met his, as if seeing him grounded her for a moment. As if she was grateful he was there.

His chest tightened. He wasn't ready for the way that felt. This wasn't the time for feelings. She was grieving. Raw. Vulnerable. This wasn't about him. But watching her navigate a moment no one should ever have to go through... something in him shifted quietly, like the click of a lock he didn't know existed.

He had wanted to show up simply to support her. To make sure she wasn't alone in this kind of pain. And he would have been content just being a steady presence in the background. But seeing her smile—even just a shadow of one—pulled something deep inside him, something he didn't have words for. Something he wasn't ready to name.

He exhaled slowly, collecting himself as her aunt walked by and touched his arm lightly, thanking him again for coming. He nodded, offering a small smile, but his thoughts were already drifting back to Jaida.

Back to the way her shoulders lifted when she laughed softly at something Monday said. Back to the way her eyes glistened when she stared at her father's picture too long. Back to the way she kept checking on her mother, always with gentle hands, always making sure she wasn't spiraling into grief alone.

Jackson's heart pulled again, tightening with an ache he didn't know how to suppress. He didn't know where this was going—or if it was going anywhere at all.

But he knew one thing for certain: He would show up for her again. And again. And again. As long as she needed. And maybe even longer. Even if he couldn't yet admit—to her or to himself—just how much she already meant to him.

A couple of days later, when Jaida and her mother stepped inside the funeral home, the warmth of the place stopped them in their tracks. It wasn't cold or impersonal the way Jaida expected. Instead, a soft, almost reverent quiet settled over the space—like stepping into an old library or a beautifully preserved historic home, where everything whispered calm instead of sorrow.

The lobby was softly lit, no harsh overhead lights, just warm sconces and shaded lamps that cast gentle pools of gold along the walls. The carpets were thick enough to soften every footstep, muting the sound so the whole place felt padded with calm. A faint scent of sandalwood lingered in the air—not overpowering, just enough to ground the senses.

Framed landscape paintings lined the hall, scenes of quiet lakes and sunlit meadows—images chosen, she realized, not to be beautiful, but to be soothing. Chairs upholstered in earth tones sat in small clusters, arranged more like living room corners than waiting-room rows. There were tissues tucked neatly into every corner, but not in a way that felt clinical; more like someone had thought ahead, knowing emotions could sneak up without warning.

The temperature was warm enough to feel comforting but cool enough not to overwhelm, and the soft hum of the heating system filled the silence in a steady, unobtrusive way. It was a place designed to hold grief gently—not erase it, not push it aside, just cradle it.

Even knowing why they were there, Jaida felt an odd sense of being welcomed—as if the building itself understood what people walked through its doors carrying.

The funeral home had the stillness of a place meant for the dead, yes—but also the warmth of a place meant to protect the living while they said goodbye.

A man stepped forward as soon as Jaida and her mother crossed the threshold—tall, neatly groomed, and dressed in a suit so crisp it could've been cut from the pages of a catalog.

Casket sharp, Jaida thought despite the heaviness in her chest, the kind of sharp that felt both intentional and a little ironic in a place like this.

His tie was perfectly knotted, his shoes polished to a mirror shine, but it was his expression that mattered most—a gentle, practiced calm that made it clear he'd guided countless families through this same impossible moment.

"Mrs., Miss," he greeted them with a soft nod, voice low and steady, the kind of voice meant to steady others. "Thank you for coming. If you'll follow me, we'll head to a private room where we can discuss the arrangements."

He stepped to the side with a small, respectful gesture of his hand, inviting them down a quiet hallway lined with muted artwork and warm lighting. The carpet cushioned their footsteps as they followed him, each step pulling them deeper into the reality of what they were here to do.

Jaida walked beside her mother through the narrow hallway, each step heavier than the last, until they were ushered into a softly lit conference room with beige walls and a round table that felt far too formal for grief.

It wasn't until the door to the private planning room closed gently behind them that Jaida felt the true weight of the moment settle across her shoulders.

They sat down, her mother clasped her hands in her lap as the funeral director began asking questions. Cremation. Service. Obituary. Program design. Words that shouldn't have belonged in the same sentence as her father's name. Words that didn't feel real.

The funeral director had a kind of quiet presence that made the room feel less sharp around the edges. When he spoke to Jaida and her mother, his voice stayed low and steady—never rushed, never clipped, never carrying that rehearsed sympathy some people used to fill silence. His words felt measured, like he understood that everything he said had to land gently.

He kept his hands folded in front of him most of the time, not in a stiff, formal way, but in a way that showed restraint—showed that he was there to guide, not to intrude. When he needed to explain something, he moved slowly, giving them time to follow, to breathe, to fall apart if they needed to.

He repeated information without a hint of impatience when Jaida's mom asked the same question twice. He waited through long pauses, letting her gather herself, never pushing the conversation forward before she was ready. Even when her voice wavered or when she seemed overwhelmed by details, he simply nodded, softening his expression as if to absorb some of the weight she carried.

With Jaida, he was just as gentle. He didn't look at her like someone who needed to take charge, even though she clearly had been. Instead, he offered choices quietly— "We can do this today, or wait until you're ready... I'm in no hurry." He explained the next steps with care, always asking, "Does that feel okay?" before moving on.

He never filled the silence with platitudes. He let it exist. He let *them* exist in it.

The whole time, his presence felt like a soft, steady anchor— a reminder that even in the most painful moments, there were still people who knew how to move slowly, respectfully, patiently. People who didn't rush grief.

Her father had always been clear about what he wanted— simple, dignified, nothing extravagant. So, they honored that. They selected a silver urn with a subtle etched design, something he would've actually liked. Then they chose a few memorial necklaces for a small portion of the ashes—one for her mother, one for her. Small, understated pieces meant to hold something priceless.

But they weren't alone.

A spokesperson from her father's side of the family sat stiffly across the table, arms folded, jaw tight, making her presence known with every pointed sigh and uninvited opinion. She talked about what "the family" wanted—none of which reflected what Jaida's father had ever asked for. No offer to help pay for anything. No willingness to contribute. Just wants. Demands.

Hands out.
Always taking.
Never giving.

The spokesperson had leaned over the table, studying the display of memorial jewelry with far too much entitlement for the moment. She tapped the 14-karat gold necklace—a delicate piece meant to hold ashes.

"I want this one," she said, not a hint of hesitation. Then she turned to Jaida, her eyes sharp, as if daring her to object. "I thought you all were paying for this."

Jaida met her stare evenly. "No," she said, voice steady but firm. "We're not."

The woman's lips thinned, irritation flashing in her eyes, but she didn't push further—yet.

As the meeting dragged on, she found her next opening.

"We should add a limo," she announced suddenly, sitting forward like she was laying down a challenge rather than planning a funeral.

The funeral director shifted quietly, his gaze moving to Jaida's mother to confirm the request. He stayed composed, but Jaida saw the flicker of unease behind his professionalism.

Her mother didn't flinch. Her voice was soft but unwavering. "And do you have the money for that?"

The spokesperson waved her hand dismissively, as if discussing something trivial. "Well… you're the wife. You can handle it."

Both Jaida and her mother went still. The director's eyes widened a fraction—almost like even he couldn't believe she'd said that out loud.

"No," her mom answered, her voice soft but unshakable, her hands curling into small, controlled fists in her lap. One word. Final. Unmovable.

That single refusal detonated the spokesperson's temper.

She shoved her chair back, the legs screeching against the floor, and raised her voice—sharp, accusatory, loud enough that staff at the desk outside froze mid-task.

The air thickened with the crackle of conflict, but Jaida and her mother didn't rise to meet it. They sat firm, weathering the storm with a quiet, exhausted dignity.

The funeral director had seen enough. With a calm nod to a staff member near the doorway, he signaled for help.

Two employees approached—polite, professional, but unmistakably firm—and gently guided the spokesperson out of the room as she muttered protests under her breath.

When the door finally closed behind her, the silence that followed felt like exhaling after holding a breath too long.

The door closed. Silence returned. Heavy, exhausted, sacred.

When they finished the final arrangements and returned home, Jaida's mother walked ahead to unlock the door. The first shock wasn't the quiet—it was the darkness.

She flipped the light switch.
Nothing.

She tried again.
Still nothing.

A frown creased her brow as she moved quickly to the kitchen and twisted the stove knob. No spark. She turned on the faucet. The water sputtered, ran weakly, then died with a hollow gurgle.

"What...?" her mother whispered, more to herself than to Jaida.

She reached for her phone with trembling fingers and dialed one of the utility companies. Jaida stood beside her, listening to the faint clicks and automated prompts before the call finally connected.

"Hi," her mother said, trying to sound composed. "I'm calling about my service—my lights aren't on, and I'm not sure why."

A pause on the other end. The kind of pause that made your stomach tighten.

"Yes, I see the account..." the representative finally said, voice cautious. "We received a call earlier informing us that the account holder had passed away. We were instructed to discontinue service."

Jaida's mother pressed a hand to her forehead. "Who called? Who told you that?"

"I—I'm sorry, ma'am. I don't have that information. But the request was processed as an urgent termination."

As if she had already ceased to exist.
As if the home didn't belong to both of them.
As if her grief wasn't enough.

Her mother hung up slowly, the phone lowering from her ear like it suddenly weighed fifty pounds.

"They called the companies," she whispered, voice paper-thin and shaking. "His family. They told them he had passed, and..." Her breath hitched. "They acted like I'm not still living here. Like I don't matter."

The house felt colder then—emptier, violated. A place that should have been their refuge now felt like another wound.

Jaida stepped forward, wrapping her arm around her mother's shoulders, pulling her in gently.

"They don't get to take anything else from you," she murmured. "Not your home. Not your peace. Not anymore."

It was the kind of betrayal that didn't just hurt—it hollowed you. A wound that scraped along the inside of the ribs instead of the skin. Losing him was devastating enough, but the way his family moved to erase her mother—as if the decades she spent in that house didn't count, as if her marriage had ended not with his last breath but with their convenience—made the grief feel sharper, more jagged.

Chapter Nine

Permission to Fall

Morning crept in quietly. The kind of gray light that made the whole world feel suspended—too still, too soft for a day like this.

Jaida stood in front of the bathroom mirror, fastening the delicate necklace her father had given her years ago. Her hands trembled just enough for her to notice. She pressed her palms against the cool dresser, closed her eyes, and breathed once... twice... trying to gather the pieces of herself she needed to make it through the next few hours.

In the hallway, she heard her mother moving—slow, deliberate footsteps, the rustle of fabric, the soft click of a jewelry box. Grief had made everything quieter in the house, even their movements.

When Jaida stepped out, her mother was standing near the front door in a black dress, one hand braced on the wall as if steadying herself. The sight of her—the strength she was trying so desperately to hold together—pulled at something deep inside Jaida.

They met in the middle of the hallway. For a moment, neither spoke.

Her mom reached for her hand first, fingers cold, grip firm. Jaida took it immediately, intertwining their hands, matching the pressure. Their foreheads nearly touched.

"We can do this," her mother whispered, voice low, steady but fragile around the edges.

Jaida nodded, eyes burning. "We can," she echoed, the words barely more than breath.

They stood like that for a beat—two women holding each other up, refusing to fall apart before the world could see it.

Then her mother squeezed her hand one more time and let go.

"Ready?" she asked softly.

"No," Jaida admitted, pulling in a shaky breath. "But I'm going anyway."

A tender, raw smile flickered at the corner of her mother's mouth. "That's enough."

They gathered their things: keys, tissues, their programs tucked neatly into Jaida's bag. When they stepped outside, the morning air wrapped around them—cool, damp, smelling faintly of dew and last night's rain.

At their cars, they shared one more nod—quiet, steady, full of meaning. Another unspoken vow passed between them: even in separate vehicles, they were still moving through this together. They could handle this. And they would.

The funeral came like a storm front rolling in—heavy, gray, inescapable. Black clothes rustled as people filtered into the church, their faces blurred by tears or hardened with something colder. Judgment. Curiosity. Grief that didn't look like hers.

Jaida sat shoulder-to-shoulder with her mother in the front pew, their hands clasped so tightly they might as well have been fused. A unit. A fortress. The only stable thing in a room full of shifting emotions.

When her name was called, she rose. Her legs felt stiff, as though grief had soaked into the tendons, but her steps were steady as she walked to the podium. The murmurs faded. A hundred eyes fixed on her.

"My father," she began, her voice soft but clear, "was a man of quiet strength. He didn't need to tell you he loved you—he showed it. In the way he treated people, in the lessons he gave, in the respect he carried for everyone he met."

Her throat tightened, but she breathed through it.

"He taught me what kindness looks like. What it means to stand tall. To keep your word. To give without keeping score. He wasn't perfect—but he was real. And he was good."

She paused, letting the silence settle around her like a held breath.

"Look to your left. Look to your right. Look behind you, and in front of you. We are his legacy. All of us. And it's up to us to carry forward the lessons he lived."

A ripple of emotion passed through the congregation—soft nods, quiet tears, a few bowed heads. Her father's life echoed in the room more honestly than any eulogy could capture.

When she stepped off the podium, Jackson was waiting in the aisle. He didn't touch her—didn't assume—but the way his eyes held hers was reassuring, like stepping onto solid earth after hours of drifting.

He leaned in just enough for her to hear him. "That was beautiful," he murmured. "He'd be proud."

And, for the first time since the catastrophe, Jaida let herself believe those words might be true.

At the graveside, after the final prayers and the low mechanical groan of the urn being lowered into the ground, people began to drift away. Feet crunched over gravel, whispers floated on the cold air, car doors slammed in the distance. Jaida's mother was gently steered toward relatives offering hugs, hands, condolences.

But Jaida stayed. She remained rooted near the fresh mound of dirt piled next to a portrait of her father, the gray sky hanging low overhead. The wind cut through her dress, but she barely felt it.

The canopy of gray sky stretched over the cemetery, heavy and unmoving, as if even the weather refused to pretend today was anything but grief. The earth beneath her shoes was soft from last night's rain, giving slightly with each step, and the scent of wet soil and cut grass mixed with the faint sweetness of the flowers people had brought.

For days, she had held herself together with the thinnest threads—steady for her mother, composed for the funeral home, firm when making decisions, calm when the world kept asking her questions she didn't have the heart to answer. But now, with the urn lowered and the pastor's final words fading into the cold November air, the pressure inside her chest gave way.

Only when the cemetery thinned, did she finally release the breath she'd been holding.

Jaida's knees buckled before she realized she was sinking onto the damp grass. Her hand brushed the top edge of the grave marker, the stone cool against her palm, and that single physical contact shattered whatever wall she had left. A sob tore out of her—raw, trembling, too loud in the stillness—but she didn't try to swallow it, didn't try to quiet it, didn't try to be strong.

For the first time since everything shattered, she let her face crumple, let her breath hitch and break, let her shoulders shake with the weight she'd been carrying alone. Tears blurred everything—the grass, the grave marker, the people in the distance—but she didn't wipe them away. She *let* them fall.

She felt the pain in waves: the sharp sting of loss, the dull ache of absence, the hollow, echoing grief of knowing there would be no more birthdays, no more phone calls, no more familiar laugh rumbling through the house. She felt the regret, too—every moment she wished she could change, every what-if she had swallowed in the name of being strong.

Here, no one was depending on her. No one was looking to her for answers, or direction, or calm. Her mother wasn't watching, trembling and fragile. Her relatives weren't hovering. The world wasn't asking anything from her.

Here, at the edge of fresh earth, she finally had permission to fall apart. So, she did.

She pressed her forehead to the back of her trembling hands and let the grief pour out of her in a way she hadn't allowed since the moment everything happened. Each sob felt like something being pulled from deep within her—a part of her love, her history, her childhood—breaking loose and tumbling into the open.

And for the first time, in this small, sacred corner of the world, Jaida let herself mourn her father fully. She didn't try to be strong. She didn't have to.

She pressed her palms into the earth as if she could reach him that way. Tears ran hot and unrestrained down her cheeks, but she didn't wipe them. They belonged to this place.

"Why did you leave me, Dad," she whispered, forehead touching the cold soil. "I still needed you."

Every mask she had worn—dutiful daughter, steady support system, shield against his family's cruelty—cracked wide open. For the first time, she let herself be small. She let herself be shattered.

Memories surged like a tide:
Her tiny hand tucked into his as they walked to the corner store for candy.
The deep, warm laugh that always found her in a crowd.
Their "dates"—Saturday dinners at whatever restaurant she chose, then a movie, or a slow walk through the park with stories about his own childhood.
And always, the sunsets.

He used to say that sunsets proved endings didn't have to be ugly.

Now, Jaida couldn't drive past her parent's house without her chest tightening. The porch felt like a shrine she couldn't bear to step onto. Every evening sky felt like a blade—beautiful, but unbearable.

She couldn't even bring herself to drive past the park where they hiked together. The moment she neared it, the memory of him dying surged back. The ache that followed was instant and piercing, as though her body recognized the grief before her mind did.

"It wasn't supposed to be like this," she sobbed, fingers curling into the dirt. "You were laughing that morning. You were *alive*. And then you were just…" Her voice broke. "Gone."

A sudden loss. No warning. No time to prepare. No chance to say goodbye. A cruelty she wasn't sure she'd ever understand.

Behind her, a presence gathered—warm but cautious Jackson. He didn't speak. Didn't offer clichés or comparisons. He had lost his mother a couple years ago, and she knew that grief lived quietly inside him, but his loss came with a long goodbye. Slow. Expected. Anticipated, even if painful.

This was different, and he didn't pretend otherwise. He simply stood behind her like a watchtower, his hand brushing her upper back every so often—light, respectful, reminding her she wasn't alone without trying to pull her out of her grief. And strangely, that restraint was its own kind of comfort.

When her sobs softened into trembling breaths, he extended his hand—not pulling, not urging. Just offering. Jaida reached for it, her fingers finding his, and let him help her to her feet. For the first time since her father's death, the world felt just a fraction less unbearably heavy.

When Jaida finally rose from the graveside, her fingers still laced with Jackson's, the world felt strangely muted—like the wind itself was holding its breath. Her legs were unsteady, her body heavy with the kind of exhaustion that grief carves straight into bone.

When she looked up at him, their eyes locked, and everything inside her shifted. In Jackson's gaze, she saw safety—quiet, unwavering, unconditional.

In hers, he saw it all: the pain she'd swallowed, the cracks she'd hidden, the breaking she could no longer hold together.

She stepped closer, her body acting before her mind could catch up. One more step, and her forehead brushed his chest. Then she folded into him completely, her head sinking against him as if his chest were the only solid thing left in her world.

Jackson wrapped his arms around her—slow, deliberate, protective. He didn't say a word. He didn't rush her grief or fill the silence. He simply held her.

Her breaths came unevenly at first, her shoulders trembling. His heartbeat was steady beneath her cheek, grounding her in a way nothing else had since the moment she got the call. He kept one hand at her back, the other lightly cupping her upper arm, his warmth surrounding her as her walls finally came down.

When she eventually pulled back, she didn't lift her head. She stood upright again, but her gaze dropped to the grass, her shoulders curled inward like she was trying to make herself small.

Jackson kept one hand on her arm—warm, steady—and with the other, he gently brushed the tears from her cheek, the ones that had soaked into his shirt seconds earlier.

Then, with quiet tenderness, he lifted her chin between his fingers. She met his eyes again, and the compassion she saw there nearly undid her. "Let me take you home," he murmured. Jaida managed a small nod.

He led her to the car, not rushing, not pushing—just staying right beside her, matching her pace. When she slid into the passenger seat, the scent hit her: Black Ice. Sharp, clean, familiar. It reminded her of car rides that didn't hurt, afternoons that didn't end in heartache.

The drive was silent.

Jaida stared out the window, watching the world blur into soft streaks of gray and green. Jackson didn't disturb her quiet. Instead, he reached over and switched the radio station until the soft, nostalgic wash of '90s R&B filled the car—Xscape, Boyz II Men, Aaliyah. He knew what she loved. He always paid attention.

He didn't try to talk. Didn't offer empty comfort. He understood silence—he'd lived in it after losing his mother a few years back. He remembered saying almost nothing to anyone, especially his father, because grief made words feel too heavy to carry.

So he let her have this. A quiet car. A safe presence. No expectations.

When they pulled into her driveway, he turned the engine off and stepped out. Before she could reach for the handle, he was already opening her door. He extended his hand, palm steady, fingers warm.

She placed her hand in his, letting him help her out of the car. Her legs felt unsteady all over again.

"Come on," he said softly. "I'll walk you to the door."

They walked slowly up the path—slow enough that she set the pace, unhurried and fragile. Jackson didn't guide her; he followed her lead, simply staying beside her, steady as a shadow.

When they reached the door, she dug her keys out with trembling fingers and unlocked it. The door creaked open, warm light spilling out onto the dark porch.

Before stepping inside, she turned back to him.
"Thank you," she whispered, her voice thin, almost breaking.

He shook his head gently. "You don't have to thank me." His voice dropped even softer. "And remember—I'm only one call away."

Her lips curved into the smallest smile, a tired one, but real. She nodded, stepped inside, and closed the door gently behind her.

On the other side, Jackson waited just a moment—as if making sure she truly made it in safely—then turned and walked back to his car. He slid behind the wheel, glanced once more at the house, and drove off into the quiet night.

After Jaida stepped through the front door, the weight of the day instantly began pressing down on her like a heavy cloak. She kicked off her shoes, the click of heels against the hardwood echoing faintly in the empty house. Slowly, methodically, she began to shed the layers of black fabric she had worn for the funeral—the blazer, the dress, the scarf— each piece a reminder of the grief she had carried, the composure she had forced herself to maintain.

Her phone buzzed sharply on the counter. **Monday.** Jaida glanced at it but didn't move. She wasn't ready for conversation, for condolences, for any words at all. She let the call go to voicemail, her thumb hovering briefly before dropping it back onto the table.

She walked into the bathroom and turned the faucet, adjusting the shower to the perfect warmth. Steam began to curl up, fogging the mirror, carrying with it a hint of lavender from the body wash waiting at the edge of the tub. She stepped under the water, letting it cascade over her shoulders, washing away the stiffness of hours spent in grief and ritual.

Closing her eyes, she imagined herself somewhere entirely different. The warmth of the sun on her skin. The gentle lap of turquoise waves against soft sand. Jamaica. The Caribbean Sea. She let herself float in that memory, or maybe a fantasy—she couldn't quite tell the difference. Every droplet of water felt like it was carrying her farther from her reality, farther from the calls, the questions, the expectations.

She had no intention of returning yet. Not to the world, not to the obligations, not even to Monday.

For now, she would linger here, in the embrace of warm water and imagined sunlight. Letting herself breathe, letting herself exist somewhere that didn't ache.

Chapter Ten

The Weight of Grace

The morning after the funeral, Jaida went to visit her mother. Her parents' house was quiet in a way that made her chest ache.

Sunlight filtered through the blinds, casting long, slated shadows across the carpet, the table and the worn sofa. The flowers from the service still sat on the dining room table, their sweet scent mingling with the faint aroma of coffee gone cold hours ago.

Every breath she took carried the memory of that day, heavy and lingering.

Her mother sat in her father's favorite chair, posture straight but eyes tired — a woman holding herself together through sheer will.

Jaida lingered in the kitchen doorway, her body heavy with exhaustion. The days of condolences, meals, and whispered family drama had worn her down, and her mother had refused to engage in the petty arguments.

Her father's family had started showing their true colors — fussing over the will, twisting words, turning grief into greed. When they cut off the utilities to the house her parents had built together, claiming it was "just business," Jaida had wanted to explode. She wanted to confront them all, call them out for the people they really were.

But her mother didn't. She handled it all with quiet grace — a calm that demanded respect even from those who didn't deserve it. She refused to let bitterness drag her out of character.

"Your dad wouldn't want me to act ugly," her mother had said, voice soft but firm, when Jaida tried to step in. "He'd want me to keep my peace." So she did. Even when she went out of her way to give one of his cousins something that wasn't listed in the will — a vintage watch her father had always wanted that cousin to have — Jaida could hardly believe it.

"Mom, after everything they did?" she asked, frustration simmering beneath the surface. "After they cut the lights off in the middle of your grief?"

Her mother's gaze held quiet wisdom. "Baby, forgiveness is more for us than for them. I'm not giving it because they deserve it. I'm giving it because your father would've wanted me to."

That was her mother — grace under pressure, strength in silence. Jaida wanted to be like her someday, but right now she was just angry, heartbroken, and exhausted.

That evening, Monday called. Her voice came through the phone, warm and steady. "Hey, Cuz. Just wanted to check on you. How are you holding up?"

Jaida exhaled, releasing a breath she hadn't realized she'd been holding. "I'm... managing. Just got home from my parents' house. Some moments I'm okay. Others... it hits me all over again."

"That's normal," Monday said softly. "You've been strong for everybody else, but don't forget you have to grieve too, Jai. Don't bottle it all up."

"I know," Jaida whispered. "I just... don't have the energy for much else right now."

"Take your time," Monday said. "You don't owe anybody anything right now. Just breathe and give yourself some grace."

Jaida managed a faint smile. "Thank you."

They talked for a while longer — mostly small things — but even that tiny connection made her feel a little less alone.

Later that night, her phone buzzed again.

> **Jackson:** Hey, just checking in. You holding up, okay?

She stared at the screen for a long moment before typing back:

> **Jaida:** Trying to.

He responded immediately.

> **Jackson:** I'm here if you need anything. No pressure.

Part of her wanted to pour out everything — the emptiness of the house, the anger at the world, the exhaustion of pretending. But instead, she typed:

> **Jaida:** Thanks, I appreciate you.

And left it at that.

He had been there at the funeral, standing quietly behind her as she helped hold up her mother during the final prayer. At the gravesite, when her knees threatened to give out, he was the one who subtly steadied her. He didn't say much — just stayed close. That quiet presence had meant more than words could.

The next day, she called him.

He picked up on the second ring. "Hey, Jaida," his voice warm but distracted — she could hear the faint hum of office noise, papers shuffling, low murmurs of conversation.

"Hey," she said softly. "Are you at work?"

"Yeah," he replied, lowering his voice. "Just stepped out of a meeting. Everything okay?"

She hesitated. Almost said no. Instead, she whispered, "I just wanted to say thank you... for being there. At my parents' house, at the funeral, at the burial. You didn't have to, but you did."

He was quiet for a moment. Then his steady reply: "You don't ever have to thank me. I wanted to be there. You deserved to have people around who care."

Something in his tone made her throat tighten. Not pity. Understanding.

She swallowed hard. "Still... it meant a lot."

He exhaled quietly, leaning back against the office wall. "I know you're hurting. I won't crowd you, but just know — whenever you need to come up for air, I'll be right here."

Her voice broke slightly. "Thank you, Jackson."

"Anytime, Jai," he said, a soft smile in his tone.

They were about to hang up when she inhaled, a slow, shaky breath he could hear.

"Hey... Jackson?"

He paused. "Yeah?"

Her voice was softer now, almost fragile. "Do you remember... when we were in the car, and I was telling you about the physical abuse?"

Jackson's entire body reacted before his mind caught up. His grip tightened around the phone. His shoulders stiffened, jaw flexing once. His heart kicked hard in his chest.

But when he spoke, his voice stayed steady. "Yeah... I remember." A beat of confusion threaded into his tone. "Why are you thinking about that right now?"

Jaida closed her eyes, fingers brushing the edge of her blanket. She exhaled unevenly. "Because... I feel guilty."

Jackson's brows pulled together. "Guilty about what?"

She swallowed, the words catching on the way out. "For never telling my dad."

Silence pooled softly between them — not cold, not distant, just waiting.

"I didn't tell him," she continued, her voice barely above a whisper, "because I knew what he'd do. I knew he'd hurt somebody... and I knew that could put him in jail." Her breath trembled. "I couldn't risk that. I couldn't lose him."

Jackson's heart sank, a heavy ache settling behind his ribs. He leaned forward on the couch, elbows on his knees, listening with everything in him.

"And besides Monday... nobody else knew. Not really." She hesitated. "Well... there was this guy friend. He saw one of them out once. The guy was bragging about what he did to me and... my friend handled it. But other than him, I never told anybody else." Her breath hitched. "Until I told you."

Jackson closed his eyes, steadying himself. "Jaida..."

"I was ashamed," she whispered, voice cracking at the edges. "I thought he'd think less of me. Or... or blame me. Or think I was stupid for being in something like that. I was smarter than that." Tears slipped hot and silent toward her pillow. "He always told me not to depend on any man for anything. He said he wanted me to be strong, to choose myself first. And I just... I didn't want to disappoint him. Didn't want him to look at me like I failed."

Jackson breathed in, slow and deep, grounding himself before he spoke. He imagined her there, curled up, hurting, thinking she had to carry all of that alone. His chest tightened.

"Jaida," he said gently, his voice firm but warm, "you didn't disappoint him."

She sniffed, quiet. "You don't know that."

"I do." His tone didn't waver. "He loved you. He saw you. And nothing — nothing — you went through would've made him think less of you. Protecting him doesn't mean you failed. It means you were trying to keep the person you loved safe. That's not weakness." He took another breath. "And what happened to you... none of that was your fault. Not then. Not now."

Another silence fell between them, but this one didn't sting. It settled lightly, like something meant to hold, not to break.

Jaida wiped a tear from her cheek with the back of her hand. "I just wish I could've told him."

"I know," Jackson murmured. "But you told me. And I'm here. I'm not going anywhere."

She breathed out a fragile, grateful sound. "Thank you."

He smiled gently into the phone. "Anytime."

A long quiet settled between them — not heavy, just full. They both stayed there, listening to each other breathe.

Finally, Jaida whispered, "I think I'm going to try to get some sleep."

"Okay," Jackson said, voice warm. "I'll let you rest."

There was a small pause before she spoke again, softer than before. "Goodnight, Jackson."

"Goodnight, Jaida," he said, matching her softness. "I'm here if you need me."

When the call ended, she sat for a long while, phone in her hand, feeling both seen and hollow at the same time.

Jackson sat back, phone still in his hand, feeling the echo of her words settle into him — protective, aching, patient, and more certain than ever that he cared deeply... maybe more than he was ready to admit.

And in her quiet room, Jaida exhaled, letting the weight she had carried alone for too long finally loosen, even just a little.

Weeks later, life forced her to move forward, even when she wasn't ready.

Before he passed, she had planned to ask her father for help house hunting — for his opinion on the neighborhood, the yard, even which way the house faced so she could catch the best sunsets. He was the person she trusted most to walk her through something that big.

She never got the chance.

Every open house and realtor email felt hollow — another moment she'd lost.

She finally settled on a three-bedroom, two-bath single-family home with a two-car garage, finished basement, and a wraparound porch. The porch was what sold her. She imagined sitting there in the evenings, coffee in hand, watching the sunset the way she used to with him — a quiet connection she could hold onto.

Her mother came with her to sign the papers, smiling through her own tears. "He'd be so proud of you, baby," she said softly.

Jaida nodded, blinking hard. "Yeah... I was going to ask him to help me pick a house. He would've loved this porch."

Her mom reached for her hand. "Then you chose right."

They sat with it—those words, the weight of them, the truth of them. Her mom squeezed once more, then exhaled softly, that familiar steadying breath she always took when she was bracing herself to be strong for both of them.

"Baby," she said gently, "come over. I'll make dinner."

The offer wasn't dramatic. Wasn't dressed up in anything heavy. But something in her mother's voice—warm, knowing, soft around the edges—reached into a place in Jaida that had felt hollow for days. A place she had let go quiet. A place she didn't realize had been waiting to be touched.

Jaida swallowed, her throat thick. "Okay," she whispered. "Yeah... okay."

She gathered her things slowly, almost ritualistically slipping her phone into her pocket, wrapping her cardigan around her shoulders like armor she didn't want but needed.

As she stepped outside, late afternoon light slid across the pavement, warm against her skin. Her car beeped when she unlocked it, a sharp sound in the quiet that made her inhale a little too sharply.

Once in the driver's seat, she didn't start the car right away. She scrolled through her playlist until she found something familiar—something from before everything hurt so loudly.

A soft 90s R&B track filled the car, warm and slow, the kind of song her dad used to hum along with in the kitchen. The opening chords washed over her, settling into the air like a balm she didn't know she needed.

She finally shifted into reverse, letting muscle memory guide her more than focus.

As she drove, the music wrapped around her—TLC, Jessie Powell, Deborah Cox—each song blending into the next. The harmonies smoothed out the sharper edges in her chest, just enough to let her breathe without feeling like her ribs might crack.

The streets blurred past. Familiar stop signs, old trees, quiet porches. The city moved around her, but inside the car, it was just her and the music and memories floating somewhere between the notes.

By the time she turned onto her parents' street, that ache in her chest had grown—nostalgia, grief, comfort all tangled together. Her parent's house came into view, porch light already on even though the sun hadn't fully dipped yet. Her mother always did that—turned it on early, "just in case."

Jaida parked and sat for a moment, hand resting on the keys while the last chord of the song faded out, leaving the car in a soft hush. A breath. Another. Then she pushed the door open and stepped out.

Before she could knock, the front door swung open.

Her mom stood there, apron on, eyes gentle, the smell of garlic and onions drifting out behind her like a warm blanket.

"There you are," she murmured, her face breaking into something tired but full of love. "Come inside. Dinner's almost done."

Jaida stepped into that warmth—into the spices, the gentle whoosh of the stove, the familiarity of home. And for the first time in days, something inside her eased.

Just enough to feel like maybe she wasn't carrying it alone.

Jaida slipped off her shoes and walked into the dining room. The overhead light cast a soft golden glow across the table, already set with two plates, folded napkins, and a bowl of green beans still steaming. Her dad's usual seat at the head of the table remained empty — untouched, chair slightly angled like he might return at any moment.

Her mom brought out the last dish and sat across from her. For a moment, they just looked at the food, then at each other, grief moving quietly between them.

Her mom reached out her hand. "Come on, baby. Let's pray."

Jaida slid her hand into her mother's, their fingers threading together the way they always had at family dinners. Her mother's hand was warm, familiar, but trembling just faintly. They bowed their heads.

"Father God," her mom began softly, her voice steady despite the ache beneath it, "we thank You for this food, for another day You've carried us through. Lord, we ask for Your comfort, Your strength, and Your peace... especially now."

She paused, her voice thinning but not breaking.
"Continue to be with us. Continue to guide us. And thank You for the love that still fills this home. Amen."

"Amen," Jaida whispered.

They released each other's hands, the warmth lingering even after they let go.

"Go on," her mom said gently, handing her the serving spoon. "Let's eat."

Dinner unfolded in near silence. Forks clinked against plates, the clock ticked steadily in the background, and the house breathed around them — settling wood, distant pipes, the kind of stillness that grows heavier when grief sits at the table too.

Her mom glanced up after a few bites. "You like it?"

Jaida nodded. "Yeah... it's really good. Thank you."

"Mm." Her mom gave a small, grateful smile, then looked back down at her plate.

When they finished, Jaida gathered her plate. "I can help with the dishes."

Her mom was already shaking her head. "No, baby. I've got it." She stood and stacked the plates with practiced ease. "You just sit for a minute. It's fine."

Jaida hesitated, then let her hands fall to her lap.

Her mom rinsed the dishes at the sink, her movements slow and thoughtful. When she turned back around, her expression softened, tired around the edges.

"Thank you for coming," she said, drying her hands on a towel. "It was... it was nice having you here. The house gets so lonely now. Too quiet."

Jaida's throat tightened. She managed a small smile and nodded, her eyes warm but weighed down by everything she couldn't articulate.

Her mom stepped closer, brushing her fingertips across Jaida's shoulder. "I'm going to lay down," she said softly. "But you can stay as long as you want. You don't have to rush off."

"Okay," Jaida whispered.

Her mom offered her a tired but loving smile, then turned toward the hallway, her footsteps soft and slow. When she disappeared behind her bedroom door, the house settled again, quiet but not empty.

Jaida remained in the dining room, letting the stillness wrap around her — the hum of the refrigerator, the lingering warmth of her mother's hand, and the familiar, aching presence of a home learning how to breathe without him.

The faint scent of coffee and cedarwood lingered as she walked into her father's study. His reading glasses still sat on the desk, a half-used pen beside them. His favorite flannel lay draped over the chair, softened by time, still holding traces of the Saturday mornings he'd fill with coffee brewing and his cheerful, off-key Sinatra.

She pressed it to her face, inhaling. Tears came fast and unrelenting.

"I miss you, Daddy..." she breathed, the words catching in the quiet room like a thread snagged on something tender and raw.

Outside, rain began to fall — a soft patter at first, barely there — then slowly gathering into a steady rhythm that tapped against the windows like gentle knuckles. The sound filled the space around her, a soft, persistent lullaby that felt almost like someone sitting beside her, keeping watch.

Her phone buzzed against the desk.

> **Jackson:** Just thinking about you. Hope you're getting some rest.

The glow of the screen lit her face, reflecting the sheen of fresh tears. She stared at his message for a moment, her chest tightening with something that was both comfort and ache.

Her fingers moved slowly.

> **Jaida:** Trying to. Goodnight, Jackson.

A reply came almost instantly.

> **Jackson:** Goodnight, beautiful.

Her eyes closed on a soft exhale. She pressed the heel of her palm against her damp cheeks, then looked out toward the window where rain streaked down the glass in wandering lines. The sound filled the room, steady and soothing.

And for the first time in days, the loneliness loosened its grip. Not gone — not even close — but softened just enough for her to breathe without breaking.

When her tears finally eased, she draped the flannel back over the chair. Her cotton socks brushed soundlessly against the floor as she made her way through her dim room. The air felt heavier now, saturated with the smell of rain and memory.

She paused in the doorway, taking in the shadows of the home she'd grown up in — the silhouettes of furniture, the familiar creaks, the quiet hum of the refrigerator in the kitchen. Everything felt emptier without him, yet somehow every corner still held him too. His laugh. His voice. His warmth.

She stepped into the hallway, the faint light from the rain-washed windows guiding her path. On the small table sat a framed family photo — the three of them mid-laugh, sunlight caught in her father's smile.

She lifted her fingers to her lips, kissed them softly, and pressed them against the glass.

"Goodnight, Daddy," she whispered, her voice trembling but sure.

The rain answered for him, steady and gentle, as she turned off the last light and let the house settle into its quiet night.

She slipped out the door, driving home through the rainfall — headlights cutting through the dark, her heart heavy but steady.

By the time she pulled up to her townhouse, the rain had slowed to mist. She sat for a moment, staring at the quiet street, breathing through the ache in her chest.

There was comfort in having made it through another day — fragile but unbroken.

The days that followed moved slowly — grief had its own rhythm, one that didn't care about calendars or clocks.

Jaida tried to keep herself busy. Work. Errands. Calls with her mom. Anything to fill the quiet. But some nights, when everything stilled, the ache would return — sharp and heavy, settling right beneath her ribs.

The house was hushed, the kind of quiet that pressed against her chest.

When morning came, sunlight filtered through the half-open blinds, laying narrow ribbons of gold across the carpet, soft and patient in the stillness of the new day. They fell across the worn sofa, across the coffee table cluttered with old magazines, and across her hands as she held her phone. The light felt almost accusatory — warm, yet fleeting, like the energy she no longer had to give.

The faint scent of lilies and roses still lingered in the air, drifting from the funeral arrangements left behind. Sweet, heavy, and slightly wilted now, the flowers seemed to echo her own exhaustion, their petals softened at the edges as if mourning alongside her. She inhaled, and the scent wrapped around her chest, comforting and suffocating all at once.

Beyond the windows, life unfolded—cars honking, footsteps echoing, people moving—while she remained still, unnoticed.

A horn honked in the distance. Somewhere far off, a siren weaved through the afternoon air, a lonely thread of sound. It felt like another world, one she wasn't ready to step back into.

Her phone stayed close, a tether to the world outside she wasn't ready to reach for.

Monday's messages sat unread, gathering like dust in a corner of her mind.

Jackson's texts, however, were different. Gentle. Quiet. Patient.

> **Jackson:** You eat today?

She stared at the screen. The sunlight shifted, brushing across her fingers like a soft nudge, then dimmed slightly as clouds moved across the sky, the light waning like her energy. She didn't answer.

> **Jackson:** Just wanted to see how you're holding up.

A breath, a pause. He didn't demand. He didn't push. He waited.

> **Jackson:** No pressure to talk. Just know I'm here.

The vibration felt like a heartbeat, gentle against her palm, a quiet presence threading through the silence.

Somewhere deep inside, she knew she wasn't done grieving. The ache in her chest still pulsed, raw and unyielding, matching the slow droop of the rose's stems.

And though she appreciated Jackson reaching out — his thoughtfulness, the quiet steadiness of his care — she knew she wasn't ready. She needed space.

The petals of the flowers curled slightly deeper. The sunlight dimmed further, and she let it wash over her while the distant city carried on, indifferent to her silence.

Chapter Eleven

Echoes of Silence

Jaida lay curled on her side, cocooned beneath a blanket that still smelled faintly like Maison Francis Kurkdjian's Aqua Universalis. The afternoon light slanted quietly through the blinds, cutting pale lines across her bedroom wall and the edge of her pillow.

Outside, the distant echo of the city drifted in — car tires against pavement, a far-off siren, the low rumble of a bus turning the corner — all sounds that continued moving, living, while she felt frozen in place.

Her phone vibrated against the nightstand.

Monday.

The screen lit her dim room for a moment, her cousin's name glowing in soft white letters she didn't have the energy to face.

Monday had been checking in every day — voice notes at first, then shorter texts, and sometimes just a single heart when Jaida didn't respond.

Jaida stared at the phone, her eyes burning, her chest tight. She wasn't ignoring her on purpose. The weight inside her just wouldn't lift enough for words to rise to the surface.

She reached for the phone, her fingers brushing the screen... then let her hand fall back to the bed.

The call faded into silence.

Jackson sat at his desk at the Foundation, the soft, persistent vibration of the fluorescent lights overhead blending with the low current of office movement around him.

The place always carried a quiet purpose — muted conversations drifting from cubicles, the occasional clack of heels against polished floors, printers whirring somewhere down the hall. It was usually a steady rhythm that helped him settle into his workflow. Not today.

A stack of case files sat open in front of him, forms clipped neatly, highlighters uncapped and ready. His computer screen glowed with intake data, community outreach projections, and a half-written email he'd stopped typing twenty minutes ago.

Numbers blurred together, and every sentence he started fizzled out halfway.

He pressed the heels of his palms into his eyes, trying to will his focus back. No luck.

His phone sat facedown beside his keyboard, the black screen reflecting the harsh office lighting.

Every few minutes — sometimes without realizing he was doing it — Jackson flipped it over, checking for a message he already knew wasn't there. His thumb hovered over the screen each time, as if willing her name to appear. Nothing.

He set the phone back down, exhaling through his nose. The air smelled faintly of burnt coffee from the break room down the hall — someone had forgotten to clean the pot again.

A coworker laughed lightly across the open floor, footsteps passing his door as staff filtered between departments. The normalcy of it all contrasted sharply with the worry simmering beneath his ribs.

He tried again to work. He clicked into the spreadsheet. Scanned three lines. Read none of them.

He lifted a pen, tapping it slowly against the desk. The steady tick-tick-tick filled the small room before he caught himself and stopped. His knee bounced.

He scrubbed a hand over his jaw, eyes drifting toward the small framed photo on his desk — him, his dad, and his mom at a community event the summer before she passed. His father's arm around both of them. His mom smiling with tired eyes.

A sigh pulled from his chest before he could swallow it down.

He leaned back in his chair, staring at the ceiling tiles. He knew Jaida needed space. Knew grief was unpredictable, heavy, suffocating at times. But the silence — the nearly week-long, widening quiet — carved at him in ways he didn't want to unpack yet.

He cared. Too much, maybe.

His phone remained still.

The office moved around him, but Jackson felt suspended, caught between duty and heart, between wanting to step in and knowing he had to let her find breathing room inside her grief.

He flipped the phone again. Still nothing. He had sent another message that morning:

> **Jackson:** No rush to respond. Just checking on you. I'm here.

No reply.

He wanted to hold her. He wanted to take the weight she was carrying and make it lighter. But he also knew grief had its own gravity.

He pressed two fingers to his forehead, exhaling slowly. He didn't want to hover. He didn't want to disappear, either.

He felt stuck between the two.

Later that evening, Jaida had slipped into a shallow, restless doze when her phone burst to life again — sharp and jarring, slicing straight through the stillness of her room.

She flinched, blinking blearily at the ceiling before reaching for the phone on instinct.

Mom.

Her mother's name blinked on the screen, steady, patient. The familiarity of it tugged at something deep inside her — an ache, a longing, a reminder of how much they were both hurting.

Jaida swallowed, her throat tight. She pressed the phone to her chest for a moment, feeling the vibration drum against her ribs. Then, slowly, she reached out. Only to place the phone facedown on the mattress beside her.

She turned over, pulling the blanket up to her chin, her breath unsteady. She wasn't trying to shut people out. She just... couldn't hold anyone else's pain on top of her own. Couldn't form the words. Couldn't keep pretending she wasn't breaking inside.

The phone buzzed again. She squeezed her eyes shut, letting it ring, letting it fade.

A few days later, Jackson stood in the doorway of his office, staring out at the late-afternoon haze settling over the city like a thin veil.

His coworkers were packing up, laughter drifting down the hall, chairs rolling back, doors clicking shut. Normal life closing out another normal day.

He pulled his phone from his pocket, thumb hovering before he typed:

> **Jackson:** Thinking about you. Hope you're okay.

He hit send. Seconds ticked by. Nothing.

He tried to tell himself she needed time. Space. Grace. Everything her heart had been stripped of when her father died.

But every hour of silence twisted inside him — fear, worry, longing — all knotted together. He cared for her more than he knew how to explain.

And with each passing day, the urge to drive to her apartment, to knock on her door and just *be there*, grew harder to fight. But he didn't do it. Because grief wasn't something you barged into.

The room felt heavier the next morning, as though the grief had settled on her skin, sunk into her bones. Jaida lay with her back to the window, the blinds closed, the faint gray light barely reaching her.

Her phone rang again. She didn't look. Didn't reach. Didn't even lift her head from the pillow. She just turned a little farther away and let it go.

This wasn't intentional distance; it was exhaustion. Emotional. Physical. Spiritual. Her heart felt bruised from the inside, her spirit quiet, her mind fogged with memories of her father — his laugh, the heartiness in his voice, the way he sang Frank Sinatra.

Losing him felt like losing part of her foundation. And she simply didn't have room for anything else right now.

Jackson sat on the edge of his couch, elbows on his knees, staring down at his phone glowing in his hands. It had been a week since Jaida had responded to anyone, and the silence pressed in around him like a weight.

His apartment was dim, the small corner lamp casting long shadows across the room. Outside his window, the city carried on — distant traffic, faint horns, the low murmur of life continuing beyond these walls — while he remained suspended in quiet worry, caught between wanting to reach out and knowing he needed to give her space.

He typed a message slowly, carefully:

> **Jackson:** Hey. I just wanted you to know I'm thinking of you. No pressure to talk. Just… I'm here. You don't have to go through this alone.

His thumb hovered before he hit send.

The message went through. Delivered.

He waited. Five minutes. Ten. Twenty.

Nothing.

Jackson exhaled, a long, heavy breath that left his chest aching. He leaned back against the couch, staring at the ceiling. He didn't feel angry — not even a little. Just helpless. Helpless and full of a love he wasn't ready to name aloud, a love that made him want to protect her from everything, even the parts of life he couldn't shield her from.

He wanted to be her peace. He wanted to be the arms she leaned into. But he also didn't want to crowd her grief or rush her healing.

He felt suspended there — caught between wanting to show up and wanting to honor the silence she clearly needed.

His phone remained still in his hand.

He closed his eyes, whispering into the quiet: "I'm not going anywhere."

He hovered his thumb over the screen, and noticed the voicemail icon blinking faintly. A quiet reminder of messages he hadn't yet heard.

He pressed play, listening to an old message he hadn't erased.

"Son, I know you're busy. I don't want to bother you. I just... I don't want to lose you too. You're my boy. Call me when you're ready. I love you."

He listened again, the familiarity of his father's voice making his chest tighten. He hadn't called back in months. Their grief had taken different shapes — his father's slow, steady, outward, and Jackson's inward, buried under work and distraction.

Three months. That's how long it had been since he'd met Jaida. Three months of stolen glances, first conversations, late-night messages, first dates — and now something deeper, heavier, had settled in his chest.

She had told him once, after a particularly tender moment, *"Don't let too much time pass before you call him."* He hadn't acted right away. He had been careful, still in denial, still protecting himself from letting someone in. But then her father died unexpectedly. And suddenly, what she had said felt urgent, real. He couldn't ignore it anymore.

He pressed the call button, staring at the screen as if the act of connecting could alter the outcome. The line clicked, and his father's voice, cautious and warm, came through.

"Jackson?"

"Hey, Dad," he said, voice low, hesitant. "I... I wanted to call sooner, but... it's been a lot."

"I know, son. I know."

He paused, inhaling slowly. "I... I wanted to tell you about someone. Someone I've... been seeing. Her name's Jaida. She's... she's helped me feel again. Like... really feel, Dad."

There was a soft silence. "I see," his father said, not surprised, only gentle. "That's good. You deserve that, Jackson. You deserve to feel alive again."

Jackson ran a hand over the waves in his hair, uncertainty and guilt twisting inside him. "I... I don't know how to be there for her. Her dad... he just... he's gone. And I want to be with her, but I also know I need to give her space. It's... it's hard."

On the other end of the line, Jackson could almost see his father leaning back in his worn leather chair, one hand absently tapping against the armrest while the other held the phone to his ear. His voice was steady, but beneath it carried the weight of understanding from experience — years of loss, reflection, and quiet understanding.

He exhaled slowly between sentences, as if each word had to be measured and let settle in the air before moving on. His eyes, Jackson imagined, were softened with memory, tracing invisible lines through the room as he spoke, and the subtle creak of the chair punctuated the spaces between his gentle reassurances.

Even across the distance, Jackson could feel the patience in his father's posture, the care in the slight pause before each phrase, and the steady pulse of conviction that this — this love Jackson was struggling with — deserved acknowledgment, respect, and room to breathe.

"Son...", his father continued, "we grieve differently. Your mother and I... I lost her, and I grieved my way. You grieved yours. It's not wrong. And it's not weakness. But this—what you feel now—this is different. It's love. And love..."

sometimes it's patient. Sometimes it's presence without pressure. Sometimes it's just being there, quietly, waiting for her to need you."

Jackson exhaled slowly, chest tight. He wasn't ready to admit it to anyone — least of all himself — but he realized his father was right. He was in love. Terrified, stubborn, reckless in denial, but in love.

"I... I think you're right," he said softly. "I just... I don't want to mess this up. And with her father dying... it just hit so hard. Everything she told me before, about not letting too much time pass... it's all real now. I finally... I finally wanted to call you back."

His father's voice softened. "It's okay, son. You're learning. You're feeling again. And that's all that matters right now. Be gentle — with her, with yourself, with all of this."

Jackson stayed quiet for a long moment, letting the words settle. Somewhere inside, he felt the first real shift in months — the old weight of grief loosening slightly, making room for something new, something he had been avoiding: hope.

"Thanks, Dad," he finally said.

"Always, Jackson," his father replied.

For the first time in a long time, Jackson felt something he hadn't allowed himself in months: unguarded anticipation.

Jackson leaned back in his chair, letting the phone rest against his shoulder. His father's words echoed in his mind: *"Be gentle — with her, with yourself, with all of this."* It wasn't advice he could act on immediately, but it planted something. A seed of clarity he hadn't realized he needed.

"I don't even know where to start," Jackson admitted, voice low. "It's only been three months. But I... I feel like I can't... stop thinking about her. Every time I see her, or even think about her, it hits me all over again. I... I care too much. And I don't know if I can be patient enough."

His father's sigh was quiet but steady, like the calm in a storm. "Son... patience isn't about waiting. It's about presence. You don't have to fix anything. You don't have to solve her grief or hers and yours at the same time. You just... be there. The rest will follow."

Jackson swallowed hard, eyes staring at the city lights outside his window. He could feel the tension in his chest, the tightness he had carried since his mother's death loosening just slightly, replaced by a strange, unfamiliar warmth. Hope. Fear. Excitement. All tangled together.

"And... I don't want to lose her," he admitted quietly, almost to himself. "I don't want to overwhelm her, but I also can't stand being... apart from her right now."

"Jackson," his father said softly, "you're not losing her. You're learning how to love. That's always the hard part. Love isn't about timing, or avoiding pain, or even controlling it. It's about showing up — even when it scares you. And I can hear it in your voice, son... you're in love. Don't fight that. Don't be afraid of it. Just... be honest. With her. And with yourself."

Jackson exhaled slowly, a lump rising in his throat. His father's words cut through the stubborn denial he had been clinging to.

For months, he had told himself it was too soon, that three months wasn't enough, that he needed more time to grieve his own past before he could feel fully alive again. But hearing it said aloud — validated, accepted — made the walls he had built around his heart tremble.

"Yeah," Jackson said finally, voice soft. "I think... I think I'm ready. To... do it right. To... show her. Not just... not just feelings, but that I'm here. That I'll... be here. And... that I care. But, Dad, it's terrifying."

"I know it is," his father replied. "But that's what makes it real. That's what makes it worth it."

Jackson smiled faintly, a tension in his chest easing for the first time in months. He realized he had been holding himself back. Holding his emotions in, guarding his heart not just for Jaida, but to avoid opening himself to anyone, even his dad.

And now, talking to his father, hearing his words, feeling his understanding... it was like the first crack in a dam that had held him back for years.

"Thanks," Jackson said finally. "For… everything. For understanding. For… just being there."

"Always, Jackson," his father replied, and he meant it. "Always."

Jackson hung up, sitting in silence for a long moment. The city hummed quietly outside, but inside him, something shifted. There was clarity now — a way forward.

Jackson stood, looking out at the city, letting the chill brush against his face. He knew the next step. He knew what he wanted. Jaida — and the courage to finally show her, and himself, that he was present.

And maybe, finally, allow himself to love fully again.

Jackson sat back in his chair, letting the quiet of his apartment settle around him. The conversation with his dad still replayed softly in his mind, like a chord that wouldn't fade.

He picked up his phone again, thumb hovering over the dial. It was time — time to finally close the gap that had grown between them over months of grief and avoidance.

"Dad," he said when his father answered, voice steadier than he expected. "I… just wanted to call back to thank you. For earlier. For listening. For not judging. For… everything."

There was a pause on the other end before his father's warm, familiar voice replied. "Jackson… you don't have to thank me. I'm just glad you called. I've been waiting, you know?"

Jackson smiled faintly, feeling some of the weight lift from his chest. "Yeah, I know. And… I'm sorry it took me so long. I've been… figuring things out. Processing. But… I feel better. I feel… more like myself again."

"I can hear it in your voice," his father said. "That's what matters. And I'd love to see you soon — maybe even meet this special lady who's got my son feeling alive again."

Jackson felt heat rise to his cheeks, caught between embarrassment and excitement. "Yeah… I think that's a good idea. I'd like that."

"Great," his father replied, a faint chuckle in his tone. "Let's set something up. I want to meet her. She sounds… important."

"She is," Jackson said quietly, a smile tugging at his lips. "I think… you'll like her."

"Looking forward to it, son," his dad said softly. "We'll figure out a time soon. And Jackson?"

"Yeah?"

"Just… keep being honest. With her, with yourself, and with me. We're all learning, all of us. You're doing fine."

Jackson exhaled, a soft laugh escaping him. "Thanks, Dad. I really mean it. I'll see you soon."

"Soon," his father confirmed, voice warm and steady.

Jackson hung up, leaning back in his chair. The quiet was different now — lighter, charged with possibility. His grief hadn't vanished, but it had softened enough to make room for new beginnings. For love. For hope. For connection.

He glanced at the flowers resting on the corner of the counter, and his heart quickened. Today, he realized, was the day he could finally act. He could allow himself to feel fully — not just for Jaida, but for the first time in months, for himself as well.

Jackson stood and stretched for a moment, then stepped toward the hallway mirror. He tilted his head, smoothing the collar of his shirt, scanning his reflection as if reassuring himself that he looked calm, collected — presentable.

Satisfied, he turned back, grabbed the bouquet of flowers resting on the counter, and took a deep, steadying breath. He was ready. Ready to show up. Ready to take the next step. Ready to let himself be seen.

And somewhere in the quiet, he felt the faintest smile of hope stir inside him — the quiet promise that this time, he wouldn't be holding back.

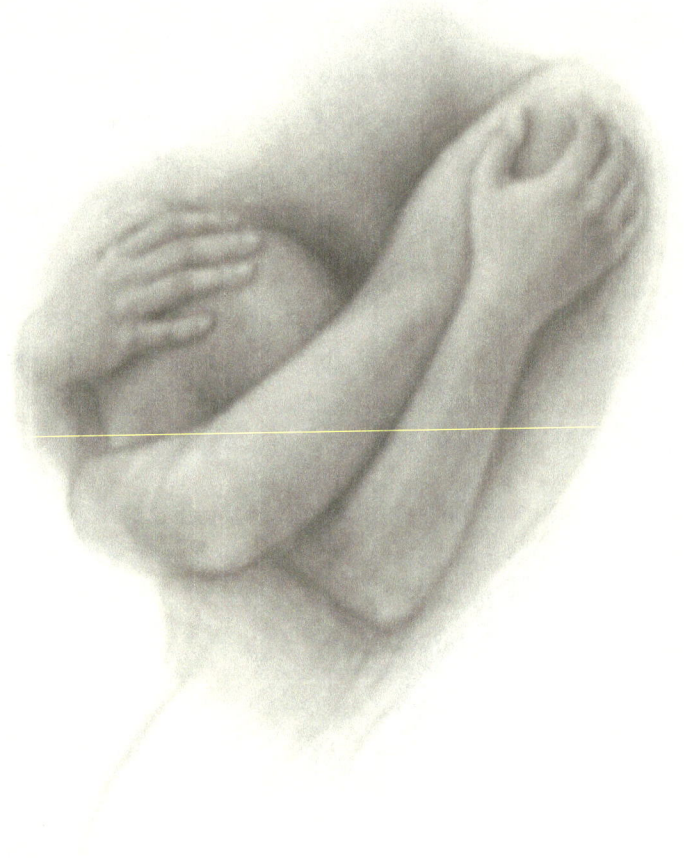

Chapter Twelve

In Your Arms

The knock came softly at first — two gentle taps that barely rose above the quietness of the house.

Jaida stirred, her body heavy, limbs sunk deep into the mattress as if grief itself were holding her there. She blinked at the dim room, the curtains still drawn, sunlight leaking through in pale slivers.

Another knock. A little louder this time.

She closed her eyes, exhaling through a tight chest. Getting up felt impossible. Like moving through water. Like lifting her whole world just to swing her legs over the side of the bed. But something — instinct, curiosity, the faintest flicker of strength — pushed her to move.

Slowly, she sat up. Her joints protested. Her heart felt too big, too loud. She ran a hand over her face, wiped the dampness from her cheeks, and forced herself to stand.

The hallway felt colder than her room. The house felt larger. Emptier. Each step was slow, as if she needed to steady herself against the walls just to make it to the front door.

When she reached it, she hesitated.

A heartbeat. Another.

Then she unlocked the deadbolt with fingers that trembled before curling around the doorknob.

Jaida's chest tightened as she opened the door.

Weeks of hiding from the world... of pacing quiet hallways and avoiding mirrors... of collapsing into bed every night with the ache of her father's absence pressing into her ribs... all collided in that moment.

Because standing there — framed by the soft gold wash of her porch light, tall, steady, and heartbreakingly familiar — was Jackson.

His chest rose once, slowly. His eyes softened when he saw her. He didn't speak right away. He didn't have to.

The sight of him alone cracked something open inside her — a breath she didn't know she'd been holding, a thin thread of relief, of longing, of fear that she wasn't ready to name. And yet... she didn't look away.

In his hands, he held a bouquet of sunflowers and deep crimson roses. The sunflowers were vivid and alive, their golden faces lifting brightly even in the dim glow of the porch. The roses were lush and velvety, the kind that drew the eye and softened the air around them — warm, intentional, full.

Jaida's thoughts flicked past him, landing on the vase resting on the kitchen counter. The vase of funeral flowers still sat exactly where she'd left it—petals curled inward like they were protecting their own grief, edges browned and brittle. The stems sagged in cloudy water she hadn't touched in days.

When she focused back on Jackson, the contrast struck her so sharply it tightened her throat: behind her, decay and silence... and in his hands, color and warmth.

"Hey," Jackson murmured, his voice soft enough to steady her. "I brought these for you."

"Jackson..." she breathed, emotion rising too quickly, too raw.

He adjusted the bouquet slightly, as if offering not just flowers but an anchor. "I remembered," he said quietly. "Sunflowers because they always made you smile. And the roses... because they symbolize the love between you and your dad. So, I thought... maybe you should have both tonight."

The words landed in her chest like a gentle blow— unexpected, tender, almost too much to hold.

She reached out, fingertips brushing the cool crinkle of the wrapping, then the warm, velvety petals. The sunflowers felt like a handful of sunlight; the roses felt like the past reaching forward to touch her.

"They're... beautiful," she whispered.

But even as she held them, her eyes drifted again to the wilted arrangement on the counter—the flowers born of condolences, heaviness, finality. And now, in her arms, something alive. Something hopeful. Two worlds brushing against each other for the first time since her father's death.

The shift inside her was small but undeniable. A place where sorrow and comfort quietly met.

"I thought you might like them," Jackson said, his voice low, almost hesitant. "And I was hoping… maybe we could get out of the house tonight. Just you and me. A little dinner, some music. Nothing fancy, just… us."

As he spoke, his gaze drifted past her, catching on the vase sitting on the kitchen counter. The wilted roses slumped over the rim, their petals crisp and defeated.

His expression softened instantly. His shoulders lowered a fraction. Something warm and aching flickered in his eyes. He didn't comment, didn't try to fix it—just absorbed what he was seeing, and in doing so, understood more of her grief.

It settled between them like a shared breath, unspoken but deeply felt.

"Jaida…" he said gently, returning his gaze to Jaida

 and stepping close enough for his warmth to reach her. "I'll wait. No rush. Only if you feel like it."

She nodded, her throat tight. "Okay," she whispered. "I'll go. But I need a minute—just… a shower."

Jackson stepped inside the house, easing the door shut as if careful not to disturb her grief. A small smile tugged at the corner of his mouth. Not pushy. Not pitying. Just steady. "Take all the time you need. I'll be right here."

She slipped away, down the hall, closing the bathroom door behind her. The shower knobs squeaked softly, and a moment later water began to drum against the tile—steady, cleansing, almost loud in the hush of the house.

Jackson stepped into the living room. He set the new bouquet on the kitchen counter, the sunflowers lifting their bright faces toward the ceiling as though trying to pull light into the dim space. Beside them, the wilted funeral flowers leaned in defeat.

He looked at the two arrangements together—life beside loss, color beside exhaustion—and something tightened in his chest. He reached out and gently straightened one of the fallen stems, not enough to fix it, just enough to honor it.

Then he settled onto the couch. He placed his hands loosely in his lap, legs still, posture relaxed but alert, like he was holding space rather than waiting. Occasionally his eyes flicked to the hallway, listening for her steps, the murmur of the water drifting beneath the door.

He didn't rush. Didn't fidget. Just stayed—quiet, patient, present—while the woman he cared for tried to pull herself together behind a closed door, grief still clinging to her like a second skin she couldn't shed.

Steam curled around Jaida as she stood beneath the hot water, her palms pressed flat against the cool tile. It was her first real shower in days—maybe longer. Time had blurred into something slow and heavy since she'd taken time off work, since she'd stopped leaving the house, since grief had turned everything muted.

She uncapped her Salt XO *Erotica* shower gel, and the scent rose instantly—jasmine oil warm and velvety, bright orange-peel extract cutting through the fog that had settled in her spirit. The fragrance filled the bathroom, wrapping around her like a reminder of who she used to be—soft, sensual, alive. She closed her eyes, letting it wash over her, letting it touch parts of her she'd forgotten how to feel.

She still wasn't happy. Still wasn't whole. But under the hot stream, with jasmine filling her lungs, she felt something tiny begin to stir—a flicker of herself waking up.

By the time she stepped out, the mirror was fogged completely, and her skin felt warm, her breathing steadier.

She moved slowly, deliberately, choosing a dress that felt gentle against her body. The fabric draped softly yet still traced the curve of her waist, the slope of her hips—subtle but undeniable. She pulled her hair into a loose ponytail, the ends damp against her neck, and looked at herself. Not healed, but present. Not okay, but trying.

When Jaida finally stepped into the living room, Jackson was sitting forward on the couch, elbows on his knees.

The moment he saw her, something in him stilled.

His breath stopped first. Then his thoughts. Then everything else.

Because she was... stunning. Not in a loud, deliberate way—she didn't even look like she knew she was. But the dress skimmed her curves in a way that made his chest tighten, tracing the soft line of her waist, the gentle sway of her hips. Her skin glowed from the steam, her damp ponytail resting over one shoulder, and the faint scent of jasmine and citrus drifted toward him with every step she took.

But more than that—she looked like she was fighting her way back to herself. And that nearly undid him.

"Wow..." The word slipped out before he could stop it, soft but reverent. Then, recovering slightly, he said softly, "You look incredible."

He stood slowly, not wanting to overwhelm her, but unable to hide the warmth spreading through him. When he stepped close, the cedar and spice of his cologne mingled with the jasmine and orange on her skin, creating a warm, earthy-sweet scent that tugged at him.

"I feel lighter," she said quietly, brushing her fingers against his. "Just a little."

He swallowed, his voice rougher when he answered, "Good. You deserve that."

Her fingertips slid into his palm, warm and delicate, and he closed his hand gently around hers—steady, protective, grounding.

They stepped out together, hand in hand, the cool evening air brushing against their skin. As the door softly clicked closed behind them, Jackson's gaze lingered on Jaida for a bit, taking in the curve of her smile, the warmth in her eyes, the way she fit against him. One clear, unshakable thought ran through his mind: *I'll do whatever it takes to keep her safe, to make her feel this alive, every single day.*

He'd been waiting for this moment—this version of her, fragile but trying, hurting but not hiding—and he wasn't letting go.

The lounge breathed with life the moment they stepped in. Low amber candlelight flickered across mahogany tables, casting warm shadows that swayed with every passing body. Soft clinks of glasses and murmured conversations blended seamlessly with the velvet-smooth notes drifting from the live R&B band onstage.

The singer's voice wrapped around the room like silk against bare skin — lush, velvety, warm — and something in Jaida's chest eased. For the first time in weeks, she felt her lungs expand fully, as if the music was reminding her how to be alive again.

Jackson reached for her hand, their fingers interlacing with gentle certainty, and then he shifted behind her, walking just a step back as if guarding her from the world. His other hand brushed the small of her back, a warm, steady guide as he followed her through the dim glow of the lounge.

Together they moved past flickering candles and low conversation until he eased her toward a secluded table tucked into a quiet corner — a place where the world felt softer, safer, and just distant enough for her to breathe.

"Sit," he said quietly, pulling the chair out for her.

He ordered for them — a pale pink floral cocktail topped with a single rose petal for her, the scent delicate and romantic; a glass of slow-burning whiskey for himself. When the drinks arrived, the candlelight glimmered off the rim of her glass like it was blessing the moment.

The band slipped into a deeper, slower groove. Across the small table, Jaida and Jackson found themselves laughing — not loudly, but freely, the kind of laughter that loosened tight places inside them. They traded playful looks over the rims of their drinks, leaned close to exchange half-whispered confessions, and every so often drifted into a quiet that felt intimate enough to be its own conversation.

But then the next song came on — *Casanova* by LeVert, the one her father used to hum under his breath while fixing things around the house or dancing playfully in the kitchen. The opening notes hit her instantly, sliding through her like a memory with a hand along her spine. Her breath snagged; her fingers went unsteady around the stem of her glass as the familiar beat wrapped around her and pulled her straight back into a moment she could no longer return to.

Jackson noticed instantly.

His hand covered hers beneath the table, warm and steady. "Hey," he murmured, voice low, anchoring. "You're okay. I'm right here. We'll get through this... together."

Her eyes fluttered closed. She tilted toward him, her shoulder brushing his, her forehead almost touching the space just above his collarbone. He didn't move, didn't rush her — just held that quiet for her, letting her lean as much as she needed.

And in that dim corner, wrapped in candlelight and soft music, grief loosened its grip. It didn't disappear, but it shifted — no longer a cage, but something she didn't have to face alone.

The drive home unfolded in a hush, the city slipping past them in streaks of gold and amber. Streetlights washed over the windshield in long, blurred ribbons, casting fleeting patterns across Jaida's thighs, Jackson's jawline, and the quiet space between them. The soft rumble of the engine was steady, almost soothing, and the night air drifting in through the cracked window carried the faint scent of rain-soaked pavement.

Jackson's hand rested over hers on the center console, warm and solid. His thumb traced slow, unhurried circles along her skin — not asking, not assuming, just being there. Every pass of his thumb softened something tight inside her, something she didn't realize she'd been holding all night.

Jaida's thoughts swirled like a tide — anticipation, fear, longing, grief all mixing into something she couldn't name. She stared out at the lights passing by, then at their hands, then finally at him.

"Do you always make people feel this... safe?" she asked, her voice barely above the quiet roll of the tires on the road.

Jackson's mouth curved, a soft tease in the shape of a smile. "I try," he said, but the warmth in his eyes held none of the playfulness — only truth. "But you..." He squeezed her hand lightly. "You make it easy."

Her pulse fluttered at the base of her throat.

By the time they rolled into her driveway, the night felt thick with possibility. Jackson shifted into park, but neither of them moved. Jaida's hand hovered at the door handle, fingers trembling just slightly.

She turned to him, meeting his gaze in the dim interior light. "Would you... come in?" she asked softly. "I don't want to be alone tonight."

He didn't rush to answer. He didn't assume. He simply searched her face, reading every trembling breath, every hint of vulnerability, every quiet plea lodged between her words.

"Only if you're sure," he said, voice low, steady — giving her an out even as he hoped she wouldn't take it.

Jaida exhaled, a breath that felt like release.
"I'm sure," she whispered.

And the way she said it — soft, certain, fragile but brave —
settled over him like a promise.

Inside, the house felt different with him there — fuller,
warmer, as if the air itself shifted to make space for
something tender. The faint scent of the fresh flowers he'd
brought earlier lingered in the living room, blending softly
with the jasmine-and-orange peel sweetness still clinging to
her skin.

Jaida stepped ahead of him, then paused. Her breath hitched
— barely, but enough — and she wrapped her arms around
herself in a quick, protective gesture. It was small, instinctive,
the kind of movement born from wounds she never fully
named. Jackson caught it instantly.

He closed the space between them slow and deliberate, his
presence steady rather than overwhelming. "Hey," he said
softly, tipping his head to catch her eyes. "You're safe with
me."

Her shoulders loosened. Something in her chest thawed at
the certainty in his voice. She reached up — almost shy at
first — and brushed her fingers against the side of his jaw. He
leaned into her touch without hesitation, warmth radiating
from him in quiet waves. She lifted her chin, breath
trembling, and their lips met.

The first kiss was soft, testing — a question. The second was an answer, deeper, hungry, alive. Heat coiled between them as their mouths found a steady rhythm, lips parting, tongues brushing in slow exploration.

Her fingers slid across his waves, pulling him closer, while his hands traced the shape of her waist, then her hips, then up along her sides with reverent patience. Goosebumps rippled across her skin wherever he touched her, especially when his lips trailed along her jaw, down her neck, then grazed her collarbone.

A quiet sound escaped her — half-whisper, half-need.

"I want you," she breathed, voice low and trembling, heat and longing threading through every word.

Jackson's chest tightened, a mix of desire and tenderness flooding through him. "You have me," he replied, voice rough with emotion, a steady, unshakable promise.

He lifted her with effortless strength, arms firm beneath her thighs yet careful — as if her body were both something he was allowed to touch and privileged to hold.

Jaida let out a soft laugh, breath warm against his neck, a sound threaded with relief, longing, and something fragile she hadn't felt in weeks.

Their mouths found each other again before he even set her down, lips colliding with a hunger that surprised them both.

He lowered her gently onto the sofa, the cushions dipping under her weight. The soft lamplight from the corner of the room cast golden highlights over her curves, the line of her collarbone, the swell of her hips. Jackson hovered above her for a moment, breath catching, eyes drinking her in, before leaning down to kiss her — slow at first, tasting the shape of her mouth, memorizing the softness of her lips.

Her palm pressed into his jaw, fingers threading through the fade at the back of his head as she yanked him closer, an urgent need driving her. A quiet moan escaped her when his lips trailed from her mouth to her jaw, then to the sensitive spot just beneath her ear. A shiver ran through her, body reacting like a hidden switch had just been flipped.

Jackson's hands slid along her back, warm and deliberate, mapping the tense places grief had carved into her. His touch was reverent, tracing every curve and dip as if learning her all over again.

She arched into him, body answering instinctively, her lips returning to his with a desperate tenderness.

When his hands slipped down to her waist, pulling her flush against him, she gasped — raw and honest, filling the quiet living room with sound.

They shifted slightly on the sofa, his body pressing over hers, breath mingling, hearts drumming in frantic unison.

Jackson paused, forehead resting against hers, eyes locking with unwavering clarity. The heat between them didn't dim, but the pause held weight — an acknowledgment of trust, desire, and the fragile intensity of the moment.

"Are you sure?" he murmured, voice low, roughened by want but steadied by respect.

Jaida reached for him, fingers curling into the back of his shirt, pulling him close until their noses brushed.

"Yes," she breathed, every syllable trembling with certainty. "I need you."

Her words settled deep in his chest — and then he kissed her again, slower this time, as though savoring the moment he'd been waiting to step into.

Clothes fell away slowly, each piece sliding over skin like a whispered permission.

Jackson's mind raced and stilled at the same time—every layer removed revealed more than her body; it revealed trust, vulnerability, the raw honesty of her grief and desire intertwined. He marveled at the courage it took to let someone in, and at the same time, he felt the weight of responsibility settle across his chest.

Every kiss, every touch, every shared breath was a conversation without words. He memorized the curve of her shoulders, the way her pulse throbbed under his fingertips, the soft rise and fall of her chest. He marveled at the paradox: she was fragile and unguarded, yet every motion, every breath, spoke of strength born from endurance.

When he entered her, it was slow, deliberate, careful—his own heartbeat loud in his ears, matching hers. They gasped together, the air between them charged with a mixture of longing and tenderness.

Her legs wrapped around him in a movement that felt natural, inevitable, pulling him closer. Jackson's hands pressed against her back, cradling, guiding, keeping her close. Moving with her in a rhythm shaped by tenderness, each movement wrapped in devotion and desire.

As he moved, he thought of her grief, the days she'd hidden from the world, the tears no one had witnessed, the weight she carried alone. And now, in this fragile, electric intimacy, he was allowed to share it with her. He leaned down, resting his forehead against hers for a moment, inhaling her scent, letting the intimacy speak louder than any words could.

Her fingers dug into his shoulders, gripping just enough to pull him closer, a silent command that made his chest tighten. Every movement, every sigh, every shiver of hers etched itself into his mind.

He wanted to be her refuge, her peace, the steady presence she could lean on—not just tonight, but always.

He moved with care, attuned to her reactions, memorizing the way her body responded, how she exhaled his name, how she trusted him completely.

And in that careful, burning rhythm, Jackson realized something profound: this wasn't just desire. This was intimacy born of trust, of shared pain, of connection that went deeper than skin.

"I've got you," he whispered against her temple, his voice low, heavy with emotion, "I've got you."

Their rhythm was deliberate, slow at first, exploratory, like two halves reacquainting themselves with a familiar language.

Every brush of skin sent shivers up Jaida's spine; every press of lips ignited heat deep in her chest. They moved together in quiet synchrony, learning, adjusting, surrendering. Her thoughts fluttered between disbelief and awe—how could someone hold her so carefully, so reverently, while also making her feel wanted in a way that left her pulse racing?

Whispers and ragged breaths filled the room, punctuated by gasps that made the walls feel like witnesses: "Yes... Jackson... right there..." Each sound, each small moan, tethered them closer—not just physically, but emotionally, a trust blooming with every shared movement.

Jaida's mind spun with relief and longing, the grief she had carried for weeks softening in the warmth of his presence.

Jackson's hands cupped her face, thumbs brushing lightly over her cheeks, grounding her in him. Every kiss carried urgency and tenderness simultaneously, a silent promise that he'd always be careful, always be present.

She traced the ridges and valleys of his chest and shoulders, memorizing the steady strength that had anchored her during her darkest days. Her fingers threaded into the textured top of his fade, tugging him closer with reflex intensity, letting him feel the desperation and trust coursing through her.

He held her like something precious, something fierce yet fragile, moving with raw, unfiltered need. Their bodies spoke in a language words could never capture—tension, release, discovery flowing in waves. Every crescendo built inevitably upon the last.

Jaida's breaths came in sharp, ragged bursts, moans growing louder, carrying her through surges of pleasure she hadn't thought possible.

Jackson's body trembled alongside hers, his voice low and rough. "Fuck" he groaned, matching her rhythm and intensity.

In that room, the world outside ceased to exist, leaving only the two of them, wholly consumed by one another.

Afterward, he pressed soft, deliberate kisses to her temple, along her cheek, tracing the curve of her neck, each one a punctuation of admiration and love. "I love you," he whispered, voice steady despite the lingering heat and adrenaline.

Tears spilled down Jaida's cheeks—not from grief, but from relief, from the joy of being held and cherished, from the undeniable proof that she could feel alive again. She pressed her lips to his in a quiet seal of shared devotion, feeling the steadiness of him beneath her.

Her fingers roamed over the planes of his chest, memorizing the ridges and curves, the quiet strength that had held her together through weeks of sorrow. *This is him. He's here. He's not leaving. I don't have to be alone anymore,* she thought, her chest tightening with gratitude and disbelief. *I can trust him. I can feel this. I can love again.*

Jackson felt the gentle press of her hands on him, tracing every line and muscle. His chest swelled with protectiveness, reverence, and a raw, aching desire. *God, she's trusting me with everything—her heart, her grief, herself...* he thought, and the weight of it only made him want to be even more present, more patient, more careful.

He brushed the tears from her cheeks, thumb lingering against the soft skin. "Shh... you're safe with me," he murmured, low and steady, the words carrying both promise and awe.

Jaida shivered at his touch, leaning into him, her mind a mixture of astonishment and relief. *I've been holding so much alone… and he's not running. He's not judging. He's here, fully here… for me.* Her fingers tightened slightly, pulling him closer, as if physical contact could tether the reality of his presence to her soul.

Jackson pressed closer, feeling the weight of her vulnerability and trust she offered freely. Every shiver under his touch, every tremor of her fingers across his chest, sent a jolt through him. *I'll never let her feel alone again. I'll hold her through all of it,* he vowed silently, his hands tracing slow circles across her back, memorizing the curve of her spine, the heat of her skin, the way she melted into him.

Their breaths mingled, ragged and warm, as hearts synced, limbs tangled, and the world outside faded.

The scent of sunflowers and roses drifted from the vase nearby, a subtle reminder of what had been lost—and what could still bloom. Grief softened into something tender, something alive, shared between them.

Jaida let herself linger in the sensation—the safety, the warmth, the intimacy. *I am cherished. I am alive. I am loved,* she realized, every thought punctuated by the rhythm of Jackson's heartbeat beneath her hands.

Jackson's gaze traced her, studying the way she moved against him, how her lips trembled after each kiss, how her chest rose and fell in harmony with his own. He pressed soft kisses to her temple, along her cheek, the curve of her neck, whispering, "I love you," his voice low, certain, full of devotion.

"I love you too," she breathed, pressing her lips to his again, letting the words sink into the spaces grief had once claimed.

They lingered tangled together, hearts syncing, limbs intertwined, savoring the warmth in the quiet aftermath. For the first time since her father's death, Jaida felt whole. Cherished. Alive. Completely, irrevocably in love.

Chapter Thirteen

Confession's Edge

Sunlight filtered through the blinds in thin, warm stripes, stretching across the rumpled sheets and drifting over Jaida's skin. The house still carried the remnants of the night before—the sweet whisper of roses and sunflowers from the vase on the kitchen counter, and beneath it all, the warm, intimate echo of shared breath and tangled limbs.

Jaida stirred slowly, the sheets brushing over her bare skin as she blinked against the soft morning light. For a split second she wasn't sure where she was—then she felt it: the steady heat of a body beside her. Jackson.

He lay propped slightly on one arm, head tilted, eyes half-lidded with sleep but already watching her like she was the first thing he wanted to see every morning from now on. When she shifted, his lashes lifted fully, a slow, lazy smile tugging at one corner of his mouth.

"Morning," he murmured, voice low and rough with sleep, the kind of voice that made warmth bloom low in her stomach.

"Morning," she breathed, instinct pulling her closer. She slid into his space like she'd been made for it, his arm wrapping around her with effortless familiarity. His body radiated a calm, steady heat—strong, balancing, safe.

Jackson reached up and brushed a stray curl from her cheek, his thumb lingering for a brief moment, soft and warm against her skin. His eyes searched hers—still gentle, still attentive, even in the first quiet seconds of the day.

"You okay?" he asked quietly, tenderness woven into every syllable.

Jaida exhaled a small, contented sigh and rested her head against his chest, feeling the slow, even rhythm of his heartbeat beneath her ear. "Yeah," she whispered, a smile curling at her lips. "Better than okay."

They stayed wrapped in the quiet for a moment that seemed to slow the world. Neither of them willing to break the soft stillness settling over the room.

Outside the window, morning unfurled in soft, gradual light, birds calling faintly from the trees, a car rolling down the street, the low stir of life beginning again.

The sunlight warmed the edges of the sheets, turning the space between their bodies into something gentle, intimate, unhurried.

Jackson shifted first, just enough to press a slow kiss to the top of Jaida's head. His lips lingered there, breathing her in— the faint scent of her skin, the remnants of last night, the warmth of her tucked against him.

"I've been thinking..." he murmured, voice still thick with sleep and something deeper. "About last night. About us..."

Jaida lifted her head, eyes still heavy, lashes brushing her cheeks as she blinked up at him. "Yeah?"

His smile was soft, the kind that curved only one side of his mouth at first before easing into something real. "I just... I really like this. Us. Being close. Everything."

Her chest stirred with something warm and weightless. She returned his smile, slow and genuine, like it grew from the inside out. "Me too. More than I thought I could."

Jackson adjusted, propping himself on one elbow so he could really see her. The sunlight caught the edges of his fade, casting a halo along his jaw. His eyes searched hers, playful but careful, hope tucked beneath the surface.

"So..." he said, a small grin tugging at his lips, "would you let me take you on another date?"

Jaida laughed under her breath, the sound soft and warm in the golden morning light. "Yes."

Relief flickered over his features, followed by excitement that lit up his eyes like sparks catching flame. "Good. I'll make it even better than last night."

She settled back against him, fingers slipping between his, fitting perfectly. "I believe you."

And with the morning quietly unfolding around them, it felt like the beginning of something neither of them had dared to imagine the day before.

Jaida lay with her cheek against Jackson's chest, listening to the steady rise and fall of his breathing. Each inhale felt like safety. Each exhale felt like a promise she wasn't sure she deserved—but deeply wanted.

Jackson held her with one arm curled around her back, his fingers tracing idle, absentminded patterns along her spine. He hadn't expected to wake up next to her. He certainly hadn't expected the quiet ache in his chest—an ache that felt suspiciously like gratitude. *She's here. With me.* The thought kept echoing through him, grounding him deeper than any morning routine ever had.

But responsibility tugged at him. His office. The grant he'd been finalizing. His mind kept circling back to it even as his body begged to stay right where he was, skin against hers, heartbeat pressed to heartbeat.

He shifted slightly, kissing the top of her head before speaking. "I've have to run to the office for a bit," he murmured, voice low, thick with sleep and something tender. "Need to finish up that grant paperwork."

Jaida didn't move right away; she just breathed him in, letting the warmth of his chest fill the space around her. She didn't want him to go—not after a night that cracked her open in ways she hadn't realized she needed. But she also loved the sense of purpose in his voice, the way he stepped into the world with intention.

She lifted her head, eyes soft, lids still heavy. "Okay," she whispered. "How long do you think you'll be?"

"Couple hours," he said, brushing his thumb along her cheekbone. "But I'll be thinking about you the whole time."

Heat bloomed in her chest—unexpected, warm, almost shy. "I'll be thinking about tonight," she admitted.

His smile widened, slow and genuine, the kind that made something low in her stomach flutter. "Yeah? Good," he said, leaning in to kiss her. It was the kind of kiss that wasn't about desire this time—it was about recognition. Confirmation. *This is real. We're really doing this.*

When he finally pulled away, he sat up reluctantly, grabbing his shirt from the floor. Jaida watched him dress, feeling a tug of longing mixed with something steadier: hope. She hadn't felt hopeful in a long time—not since the world had cracked open with loss. But now… now there was something to look forward to again. A dinner tonight. A moment to reconnect. A reason to smile before she even knew what the evening would bring.

Jackson glanced at her from the doorway, hand resting on the frame as if he needed one more second to take her in. Her hair tousled from sleep, her skin kissed by morning light, the softness in her eyes that wasn't there weeks ago. *She's healing*, he thought. *And somehow… I get to be part of that.*

"I'll see you tonight?" he asked, even though he already knew the answer.

Jaida nodded, a small, glowing smile curving her mouth. "See you tonight."

He gave her one last look—a look that held gratitude, desire, and a quiet, growing certainty—and then slipped out, closing the door gently behind him.

The room settled into stillness.

Jaida lay back against the pillows, her body still warm from where he'd been. Her mind drifted through everything they'd shared—the tenderness, the vulnerability, the way he touched her like she mattered. Tonight suddenly felt like the beginning of something she hadn't dared imagine.

As Jackson stepped into the cool morning air, the chill hit his skin, waking him fully—but it couldn't quiet the warmth still lingering from her touch. The neighborhood was just beginning to stir: a garage door rumbling open somewhere down the street, the distant bark of a dog, the faint scent of dew lifting off the grass. He slipped his hands into his pockets, exhaling a slow breath as he headed toward his car, already counting the hours until he'd be back with her.

Inside the townhouse, Jaida watched the door close behind him, sunlight spilling softly across the sheets he'd just climbed out of. Her fingers brushed the warm indentation he'd left, her heart unexpectedly full, the quiet in the room shifting in a new rhythm—less heavy, less lonely. And though they didn't say it out loud, both walked into their separate mornings carrying the same unshakable truth: *I didn't expect to feel this deeply again.*

Jackson didn't even start the car before pulling out his phone. He needed… reassurance. He needed someone who'd give it to him straight.

His dad answered on the second ring, voice warm with years of steady wisdom. "Hey, son."

Jackson leaned back in the driver's seat, thumb rubbing the wheel absently. "Dad… I went to see Jaida yesterday."

A low, knowing chuckle. "Mhm. And?"

"It was good. Better than good. She…" He paused, searching for the right words. "She let me in again. Really let me in. But—"

"There it is," his father said gently.

Jackson sighed. "If she knew the truth—everything I've been holding back—she'd run. I know she would. And the last thing I want is to lose her."

For a moment, there was only silence. Then his dad's voice came through, firm but compassionate: "Son, any relationship built on a lie—big or small—won't last long. It'll rot underneath the surface. People think lies protect love, but really? They starve it."

Jackson closed his eyes, jaw flexing.

"You've got a good woman there," his dad continued. "One who's been through hell and is finding her way back. You want to love her right? Give her the truth. Let her choose you with eyes open."

Jackson swallowed hard. "I'm scared."

"Being scared means it matters." His voice softened. "But tell her. Before the truth tells on you."

Jackson nodded, even though his father couldn't see. "Yeah… okay."

"Love you, son."

"Love you too."

When the call ended, Jackson's gaze lingered on the windshield as if the street beyond held answers. His chest ached—not from dread, but from the weight of responsibility pressing quietly against him. Tonight, he'd be honest.

Meanwhile, back in her room, Jaida finally reached for her phone—dozens of missed notifications lighting up the screen. The first name she tapped was Monday.

"Girl." Monday answered immediately, breathless, dramatic, loud enough that Jaida had to pull the phone slightly away. "Are you ALIVE? I've been calling you for days!"

Jaida laughed—a real, light laugh she hadn't felt in months. "I'm sorry. Yesterday was… a lot."

"Clearly! Now spill."

Jaida pulled the sheets tighter around her, her smile softening. "Jackson showed up unexpectedly. We… had a really good night."

Monday gasped like she'd been waiting her whole life for that sentence. "So y'all FINALLY did it? Oh thank Goodness. I don't know how y'all lasted this long. The tension between you two was stressing ME out."

Jaida covered her face with her hand, cheeks warm. "Monday…"

"What? I'm just saying." Her voice gentled. "But more important than all that—I'm just glad you're happy. That he's getting you out the house. That you're getting back to *you*."

A quiet breath left Jaida. "Yeah… I felt like myself last night. For the first time since my Dad…"

Monday's voice softened instantly. "He'd be happy for you. For this. For you letting someone in."

Jaida blinked back tears. "Jackson asked me on another date."

"Oh?! Where?"

"I… don't know yet."

"Well, wherever he takes you, wear something cute and drink water so your skin glows. And text me when you leave the house or I'll assume you're being kidnapped by love."

Jaida laughed again—warm, grounding. "I will."

Before Monday could start another tangent, Jaida's screen flashed.

"Wait—my mom's calling. I'll call you later?"

"Yes! And don't disappear again unless it's for sexy reasons!"

"Bye, Monday."

Jaida switched over.

"Hi, Mom."

"Hi baby," her mom said, voice filled with the gentle warmth Jaida had missed. "Just checking on you. How you feeling this morning?"

"I'm okay. Actually... I'm good."

A pause—then a smile she could hear. "Good. That's all I want."

In the background, Jaida heard shuffling and a familiar voice calling out.

"Is that Aunt Milan?" she asked.

"Yes, girl, she's rushing me," her mom huffed. "We're going to Pilates and then grabbing lunch. She claims I need to 'strengthen my core and my social life.'"

Jaida laughed, imagining her aunt already halfway out the door, gym bag swinging. "Tell her I said hi."

"I will." Her mom softened. "I love you, sweet girl."

"I love you too, Mom."

"Talk to you later."

"Okay. Have fun."

The call ended, and Jaida sat for a moment in the quiet— sunlight warming her skin, sheets still smelling faintly of Jackson, heart beating with something she hadn't felt in so long: Hope.

That evening, Jackson's car glided to a smooth stop in front of the steakhouse. The engine's hum faded into the evening air, mingling with the faint chatter of pedestrians and the distant clink of glasses from inside.

The valet stepped forward, hand outstretched, but Jackson barely registered him—his attention was locked on Jaida as she slowly traced on a fresh layer of lipstick in the rearview mirror, her fingers drifting over to the door handle afterward.

"Stay right there," he said, his voice low, calm, deliberate. He stepped out, the leather of his shoes clicking against the pavement as he rounded the car to open her door.

Jaida smirked, tilting her head just slightly, letting him meet her gaze. "Such a gentleman," she teased, letting her hand fall into his as she stepped out, graceful and assured.

The evening light caught her curves perfectly—her black dress hugging her in all the right places, candlelight from the entrance reflecting off the subtle shimmer of her diamond necklace. Her long, loose curls framed her face in soft waves, and the faint hint of her Baccarat Rouge 540 perfume—jasmine and something deeper, warmer—drifted toward him. She was mesmerizing, and Jackson felt a tug in his chest he hadn't expected.

He drank her in, noting the small things—the way her eyes caught his, the flush to her cheeks when she realized he was staring, the gentle curve of her smile before she met his gaze again. It wasn't just attraction; it was a quiet, steady pull he didn't want to resist.

Jackson himself was every bit the picture of control and confidence—fresh fade perfectly lined, beard sharp, Signature Bond No. 9 cologne—spices, woods, amber — drifting in the air around him. His black Louboutin's gleamed under the soft glow of the streetlights, perfectly tailored Ralph Lauren Purple Label slacks accentuating his frame, and the red Kenneth Cole shirt hugged him with just enough boldness. A black tie, straight and sharp, and the Movado watch catching light with every slight turn of his wrist. He looked good—better than good—and he knew it.

But Jaida's look—her eyes darkening with a mixture of amusement, admiration, and something unsaid—was unraveling him in a way no mirror, no careful grooming, no outfit ever could. The quiet heat in her gaze pressed against him like a tide, gentle but undeniable.

"You just going to stand there and stare all night?" she asked, a teasing lilt in her voice.

"Maybe," Jackson admitted, slow smirk tugging at his lips. "Can you blame me?"

She rolled her eyes, but the blush creeping across her cheeks was anything but dismissive. He caught it, savoring it. That small, unspoken acknowledgment—her warmth, her presence—was worth more than any arrangement of threads or cologne. For the first time that evening, he let himself feel the pull, the anticipation, the thrill of being exactly where he wanted to be.

Hand in hand, they stepped inside. The rich, savory scent of seared steak mingled with the warm, yeasty aroma of freshly baked bread, wrapping around them like a welcome. Low conversation floated through the room, punctuated by the soft clink of glasses and the occasional muted laugh, creating a cocoon of intimacy that seemed to belong only to them.

The hostess led them through the dimly lit space, her heels clicking softly against the hardwood floor. Candlelight flickered on the polished surfaces, casting shadows that danced along the walls. Jackson guided Jaida with a gentle squeeze of her hand, feeling the familiar warmth of her palm against his, a quiet tether to the moment.

As they reached a secluded table near the window, Jackson moved ahead, pulling out Jaida's chair with effortless grace. She sank into it with a soft sigh, crossing her legs elegantly, and murmured a quiet, "Thank you," her eyes catching his briefly. He pushed the chair in for her, watching the subtle curve of her shoulders relax as she settled in.

He took his seat across from her, fingers brushing against the table as he surveyed her. Candlelight kissed the angles of her face, highlighting the soft glow in her eyes and the delicate curve of her smile.

For a moment, the rest of the restaurant—the diners, the waitstaff, the gentle whisper of activity—faded into a blur. All that mattered was the warmth radiating from the woman before him.

The perfect mood—the soft lighting, the low music, the quiet intimacy—was set. Yet for Jackson, it paled in comparison to the pull he felt sitting across from her, watching the way she looked at him, the subtle play of expression on her face, the quiet joy she carried that he was finally a part of. He inhaled lightly, the scent of her perfume mingling with the richness of the room, and felt a slow, steady thrill of being exactly where he belonged.

Jackson picked up the menu, though his eyes kept drifting to her. She was scanning hers too, but every now and then her gaze would lift, meeting his, and a soft smile would curl her lips. He caught himself leaning in slightly, as if proximity could communicate what words couldn't.

"Everything looks good," Jaida said softly, voice low and thoughtful, brushing a stray curl behind her ear. "I don't even know where to start."

Jackson's lips curved in a teasing smile. "Then start with what makes you happy. I trust your taste."

Her eyes flicked to his, a mix of amusement and warmth, and her cheeks flushed ever so slightly. That subtle reaction made his chest tighten—not in desire, but in the quiet, steady pull of care. He wanted to give her everything she deserved tonight: laughter, comfort, a break from the weight she'd been carrying for weeks.

When the waiter arrived, Jackson ordered with ease, his calm presence a silent anchor. Jaida followed his lead, choosing something she'd usually hesitate over, something bold and comforting. He noticed the slight lift of her eyebrows at her own choice, and he couldn't resist a soft, approving nod. "Perfect," he breathed, and the way she smiled back at him—grateful, amused, alive—made the corners of his mouth tug upward.

Their food arrived, steaming and fragrant, but neither touched it right away. Instead, they sat in a quiet rhythm, hands brushing across the table, fingers occasionally intertwining. The hum of the restaurant faded into a background melody to their shared space.

"You know," Jaida said after a pause, "I wasn't sure about going out tonight. I... I've been so locked in my own head, it's been hard to think about anything else."

Jackson's gaze softened. "I know. That's why I'm glad you let me in. Even a little." His thumb brushed over her knuckles lightly, a gentle, grounding touch. "You don't have to do it alone."

A small, genuine smile tugged at her lips. "I know. And I... I'm glad it was you."

He caught the fleeting vulnerability in her expression and felt a protective surge. Every part of him wanted to reassure her, to hold her safe, to make sure she knew she could trust the warmth and steadiness between them. He leaned back slightly, still holding her gaze. "Then tonight... let's just be here. No past, no future. Just now."

She nodded, and for a brief moment, the weight she'd carried for weeks seemed to lift. She laughed softly at something he whispered, the sound airy and full, like a small spark reigniting in her chest. Jackson laughed too, quietly, savoring the way her eyes lit up, the way her lips curved, the way she seemed to belong fully in the world again.

As they finally began to eat, their conversation flowed naturally—stories, jokes, small confessions, teasing glances.

The intimacy wasn't just in the touches, but in the ease, the shared smiles, the comfortable silences that didn't feel empty but full of unspoken understanding. Jackson felt a quiet pride swelling in his chest. She was here. She was opening herself, bit by bit, and he was allowed to witness it, to be a part of it.

And in every moment, he caught himself thinking: *She's alive again. And I'm going to make sure she stays that way—as much as I can.*

Jackson leaned back in his chair, watching Jaida under the soft, golden glow of the restaurant's lights. Every detail drew him in—the way she crossed her legs, subtle elegance in every movement, the tilt of her head as she glanced at the menu. Effortless. Mesmerizing. He exhaled slowly, that rare, undeniable pull tightening in his chest.

Jaida caught his gaze, her eyes lifting just enough to meet his. "What?" she asked, voice teasing, a soft lilt that made his pulse skip.

"Nothing," he said, shaking his head with a small chuckle, though the weight of truth lingered in his tone. "Just wondering how I got lucky enough to sit across from the most beautiful woman in the room."

Even Jackson, confident and composed in every other setting, felt unmoored tonight. Maybe it was the way her confidence had a quiet strength, the way her layered perfume wove around him like a whispered secret. He couldn't take his eyes off her.

Jaida smirked, resting her chin in her palm. "Smooth," she said, a playful edge in her voice. "But keep talking."

Dinner flowed around them like a gentle current. Laughter mingled with quiet pauses, the kind that weren't empty but full of shared understanding. Fingers brushed lightly across the table, brief, accidental, yet electric. Jackson felt every touch, every glance, anchoring him in a way he hadn't realized he'd been craving.

She took a slow sip of her wine, eyes flicking over the rim to catch his reaction. "You always this much of a gentleman?" she teased, a small curve in her lips.

Jackson's smirk deepened, his voice dropping low. "Only when I'm trying to impress an amazing woman."

Jaida raised a brow, smirk curling wider. "So, I should feel special?"

"You have no idea," he murmured, leaning in slightly, the warmth of his words brushing against her ear as if meant only for her.

The world outside the restaurant faded into a blur—the soft clinking of glasses, the low whir of conversation, even the subtle scent of seared steak and roasted bread melting into the background. Nothing existed beyond the quiet orbit of the two of them, the intimacy of proximity, the ease of connection.

Jackson felt his chest tighten as he studied her, as if he were memorizing her all over again. Jaida was intoxicating. Magnetic. Alive in a way that pulled at him softly but relentlessly. And he knew she felt it too, the pull, the silent agreement between them that nothing else mattered tonight.

Eventually, the plates were cleared, the final sips of wine savored. Jackson didn't hesitate, sliding his card with casual ease. Hand in hand, they stepped out into the night, the warm evening air curling around them like an embrace. Jaida inhaled deeply, the scent of the city mixing with the lingering perfume of dinner, and Jackson felt a quiet surge of contentment.

He caught her gaze, the faintest smile tugging at her lips, and a knot tightened in his chest. *Tonight feels perfect… but what if it all unravels?* The thought prickled at the edges of his mind, a quiet warning beneath the warmth of the moment.

His car gleamed under the soft glow of the streetlights, waiting patiently at the valet. Jackson stepped forward, opening the door for her, and Jaida slid in with that effortless grace he could never get enough of. Her legs crossed neatly, the curve of her dress catching the subtle light from the dashboard, and he felt the familiar pull in his chest—equal parts desire and something deeper, unspoken.

The engine came alive with a low rumble, and quiet strains of soft R&B filled the car. Jaida's fingers traced idle patterns along the leather seat, and Jackson caught every flicker of movement, every subtle glance she cast his way. The air between them was thick with tension—not discomfort, but a magnetic pull neither dared to acknowledge aloud. Every brush of her arm against his, every tilt of her head toward him, spoke volumes louder than words ever could.

He kept his eyes on the road, though he could feel her watching him, the slight tilt of her chin, the curl of her lips as if she knew exactly what effect she had on him. He stole glances at her anyway, drawn in by the warmth radiating from her, the way the candlelight from dinner still seemed to cling to her skin.

The drive back was quiet, punctuated only by the soft rush of the tires on the asphalt and the occasional note of music floating through the car. Neither spoke; neither needed to. The tension itself was intimate—a conversation in glances, small smiles, and shared breaths.

When Jackson pulled into her driveway, the familiar sight felt different tonight. It wasn't just the end of the evening—it was the weight of what had passed between them, the quiet understanding that neither of them wanted to break. The world outside could wait.

He parked with smooth precision, hands steady on the wheel, though his chest thumped a little faster. Reaching across, his fingers brushed hers, a silent acknowledgment of everything unsaid. She returned a small, knowing smile, and for a heartbeat, the world narrowed to just the two of them.

Jackson's hand drifted to his pocket, pulling out the small pack. He rolled the blunt with practiced ease, the paper crackling softly in the quiet of the car. The scent of earthy tobacco and sweet herbs filled the air as he pinched it closed, held it to the lighter, and flicked the flame. The tip caught, glowing red, smoke curling upward in lazy, hazy spirals. He inhaled slowly, letting the warmth fill him, and exhaled in a controlled rhythm, letting the tension in his shoulders ease slightly.

The blunt rested in the console's holder, smoke coiling toward the roof. His hands now rested on his knees, thumbs rubbing together almost absentmindedly as he tried to steady himself. His gaze flicked to the rearview mirror, to the lines of the dashboard, anywhere but Jaida's eyes—but he couldn't hide for long.

The quiet between them held more weight than words ever could, thick with anticipation, unspoken confessions, and the pull of everything they hadn't said.

Jaida's fingers drummed lightly against her own thigh, heart hammering, mind racing. She tried to steady herself, tried to prepare for what she didn't want to hear. *Okay, Jai,* she told herself. *Stay calm. Don't react. Just listen.*

Jackson inhaled, slow and deep, letting the smoke fill his lungs before releasing it with a shuddering exhale. The movement did little to ease the tension coiling in his chest.

"I didn't think this would be so hard to say," he finally admitted, voice low, raw, almost breaking. His fade caught the light from the streetlamps as he shifted, the textured top brushing against his fingers as he nervously ran a hand through it.

Jaida swallowed, her throat dry. *That's not a good sign.* She leaned forward slightly, trying to bridge the space between them without saying a word.

"You're not going to look at me the same after this," he murmured, each word weighted, measured.

Her stomach twisted. *Here it is.* She met his eyes. "Try me," she said, soft but steady.

Jackson's hand lifted to the blunt again but hesitated, his thumb hovering over the edge. He let it fall to the console, fingers splayed on the leather as if it could anchor him. His jaw tightened, and for a moment, he seemed smaller, vulnerable in a way he rarely allowed himself to be.

"I've been trying to find the right time to tell you," he said, voice rough. "I didn't want to ruin... this." He gestured vaguely between them, the space humming with the weight of the night.

Jaida's heart thudded. She gripped her own hands, bracing herself. Whatever was coming, she was determined to meet it without fear.

"Jaida…" His voice cracked ever so slightly. And then the words came, slow, deliberate, each one a shard of hesitation.

"I—there's something you should know. About me… something I haven't told you yet."

Jaida's pulse jumped. Her mind reeled, imagining the scenarios: a lie he'd been keeping, a complication she couldn't fix. But nothing in her rehearsed fears could have prepared her for the truth he was about to lay bare.

"I… I spoke with my dad today," Jackson continued, voice catching, "and I realized… if you knew everything about me, the real truth… you might walk away. I don't want to lose you, Jai. Not after tonight. Not after everything."

Her chest tightened. "Jackson…" Her voice was soft, but the urgency behind it mirrored the racing in her heart. "Just… tell me."

He drew in a shaky breath, closing his eyes for a brief moment, as if gathering courage from the shadows of the car's dim interior. "There's more than just us I've been dealing with. Family stuff… complicated stuff… and I didn't tell you because I was scared it would push you away."

Jaida's hands unclenched slowly, her mind whirling but still tethered to him. *Scared? Jackson? Him?* Her pulse thrummed in her ears.

Jackson finally met her gaze fully, raw honesty in every line of his face. "I know I should've been upfront from the start. But I wanted to be... with you. Tonight... us. And now, I can't hide it anymore. You deserve the truth, and I—"

Her lips parted, ready to respond, to reassure him, to tell him nothing could change how she felt. But the phone on the dashboard buzzed again, a sharp intrusion, and Jackson's hand hovered for a split second before he declined it with a frustrated flick.

He leaned back, exhaling slowly, running a hand across his face. "I just... I didn't want to lose you," he admitted quietly, almost to himself.

Jaida reached out, her hand brushing his, fingers curling lightly around his. "Jackson... I need... the full story. No half-truths."

He nodded, swallowing hard. The tension between them was almost unbearable, heavy with desire, fear, and the raw pull of something neither wanted to let go.

And in the quiet aftermath of his confession, with only the faint glow of the streetlights illuminating their faces, Jaida realized this—tonight was a turning point.

Chapter Fourteen

The Storm

Jaida sat rigid in the passenger seat, every muscle taut, chest rising and falling in shallow, uneven breaths. Her heart pounded like a drum in her ribcage, each beat echoing against the weight of his words. *Did he… really just say that?*

The confession hung over her like a storm cloud, dense and suffocating, pressing down on her shoulders, her mind. Her thoughts scattered, refusing to land anywhere safe. She stared through the window, but the world outside felt unreal.

The moon draped the street in soft silver, indifferent stars blinked in the vast sky, crickets chirped in a steady rhythm, and cars passed in bursts of light, cutting through the darkness like fleeting specters. None of it penetrated her fog.

Inside the car, the quiet was deafening. The usual hum of the engine, the subtle creak of leather seats, even the lingering scent of his cologne—all of it seemed muted, swallowed by the tension that filled the space between them.

Then, a voice broke the heavy silence. Gentle, tentative, a lifeline tossed into the void of her panic.

"Jaida," Jackson said quietly, his tone low but carrying a subtle tremor, as if he, too, was bracing against the weight of the moment.

Her eyes flicked toward him, expression carefully unreadable, walls already built around her chest and heart. She didn't answer. Not yet.

"Baby, please... say something," he pleaded, voice tight, almost breaking, the desperation threading through each word like a fragile wire straining under weight.

She stared straight ahead, lips pressed together, jaw tight. Her hands clenched in her lap, nails biting faint crescents into her palms. Every muscle in her body screamed—part defiance, part fear, part heartbreak.

"Say anything," he urged again, voice cracking, low and raw, like a man unraveling in slow motion.

Jaida didn't move. Her eyes remained unfocused on the passing shadows outside the window. Inside, she replayed everything—the laughter, the touches, the stolen moments of closeness—now all refracted through the lens of his confession. Each memory twisted slightly, sharpened.

Her chest ached, and a hollow pulse seemed to echo in her stomach. She wanted to speak, to release something, anything, but the weight of shock and hurt pinned her tongue.

"Please... talk to me," Jackson said again, louder now, the words catching in his throat as he leaned slightly toward her, the space between them heavy, taut with unsaid things.

She shifted just enough to hide her face in the shadows of the car, turning inward, retreating. Her hair fell over her shoulders like a curtain, shielding him from the storm in her eyes.

Jackson exhaled slowly, painfully, raking his hands through his waves. His jaw clenched, a tension he couldn't release. The familiar rhythm of his heartbeat sounded deafening in the quiet of the car. He could feel the air itself growing heavier, thicker, almost pressing down on his chest, and with each heartbeat, the weight of her silence settled deeper, as if the space between them had solidified into something almost physical.

He wanted to reach across, to pull her into him, to erase the pause, the hesitation, the pain—but he feared that any sudden move might shatter her entirely. So he stayed still, silent for a moment, trying to summon patience he didn't feel.

The car was still, the only sound the faint purr of the idling engine and the occasional distant car sliding along the wet asphalt. The glow from the streetlights cast fleeting shadows across their faces, flickering like restless thoughts.

Jaida's eyes, sharp and unyielding now, didn't leave him. Her jaw was set, lips pressed in a line of control, but the tension in her shoulders betrayed her. She was holding herself together, but Jackson could feel the tremor of uncertainty radiating off her, subtle but undeniable.

"How... how do you feel?" Jaida's voice cut through the quiet, soft but steady, as if she were testing the air between them. Her fingers tapped lightly against the edge of the dashboard, a small rhythm that belied the storm in her chest.

Jackson froze, caught off guard. That was her first response—not anger, not disbelief, not accusation—but concern. He blinked, swallowed, and for a moment words refused him. His hand rested on the wheel, knuckles tight, tracing the cold leather. "Uh… okay, I guess," he said finally, voice uneven, awkward, like he was trying to hide the rush of emotions threatening to spill over.

Jaida watched him, the light of the moon streaking across his face, highlighting the neatly kept beard framing his jaw, and the tension in his brows. She didn't push. She waited. Just watched.

Jackson exhaled, his chest tightening, and let his gaze drop to his lap before returning to the dark street ahead.

The rain began without warning, sudden and insistent, hammering against the windshield like the world itself had decided to break open. Wipers thrashed back and forth, slicing through the golden blur of streetlights and reflections, but they could never quite keep up. The scent of wet asphalt and ozone filled the car, sharp and electric, mingling with the tension that sat heavy between them.

Jackson's chest tightened, the weight of the night pressing down on him. He gripped the steering wheel, knuckles pale, heart hammering like the rain against the glass. He wanted to reach across the space between them, to say something that would bridge the silence, but the words wouldn't come. His mind reeled with fragments—fear, longing, regret—all tangled into a knot he couldn't untangle.

He stole a glance at her, the soft silver light catching the curve of her cheek, the tense line of her jaw, and it nearly broke him. Every drop of rain seemed to echo the ache in his chest, relentless and unyielding, a storm outside that perfectly mirrored the storm inside him.

The night stretched ahead, streaked with silver and gray, unexpected, unrelenting, like the truth they'd unearthed.

He swallowed hard, exhaled slowly, and whispered into the hum of the car and rain, "I didn't tell you sooner," he admitted, voice low, thick with regret. "Because I was afraid... afraid you'd run. Afraid it would... ruin this, ruin us." He swallowed hard, the words catching. "I couldn't lose you."

Her eyes softened, glimmering with something he couldn't name—pain, yes, but also understanding. She shifted slightly, fingers brushing the edge of his arm, grounding him.

He ran a hand over his face, fingers skimming along his jaw before falling back to the wheel. The vulnerability of her question loosened the knot in his chest. "I just... I don't want to lose you," he whispered again, quieter this time, more certain, almost like a prayer. "Not now. Not ever."

The moonlight flickered across the dashboard, casting shadows that moved across their faces. Outside, the rain softened to a drizzle, and for a moment, the world beyond the car felt distant and unimportant.

The night wrapped around them—tense, fragile, intimate—but in that quiet, Jackson felt the thinnest thread of hope. That maybe, just maybe, they could navigate this together.

Jaida's breath hitched faintly, barely audible. She leaned slightly back in the passenger seat, letting her fingers rest lightly in her lap, curling just enough to fight the impulse to reach out to him. "You think lying... keeping it from me... would protect us?" Her voice, though calm, was layered with incredulity and a sharp undercurrent of hurt.

Jackson shook his head slowly, eyes flicking to her profile in the dim light, the curve of her cheek catching the glow from the streetlamp. "No... I know it's not right," he admitted, voice low, almost a confession to the night itself. "I just... I wanted tonight to feel real, not ruined by the truth hanging between us."

Jaida exhaled slowly, a sigh that trembled somewhere between frustration and understanding. "You think protecting me from the truth makes you a good man?" she asked, her words softening but carrying a quiet edge of authority.

He ran his fingers over his beard, tracing the sharp line of his jaw as if trying to map the tension coiled inside him. Each bristle scraped his skin, grounding him yet reminding him of the unrest he couldn't shake.

For a heartbeat, he lingered there, caught between the urge to act and the weight of what had already passed, before letting his hand fall back to the wheel, knuckles tight, the motion heavy with everything left unsaid.

"I thought I was... but I see now I was only protecting myself—from losing you."

A long pause stretched between them. The street outside continued on, indifferent, while inside the car the air felt taut, charged, heavy with honesty. Jaida's chest rose and fell in shallow, measured breaths, her mind spinning with anger, relief, confusion, and longing all at once.

Finally, she turned her gaze back to him, searching his eyes as if trying to decipher the man behind the words. "You're... afraid," she said, voice quieter now, a note of empathy threading through the accusation.

Jackson nodded slowly, the tension in his shoulders easing fractionally at her recognition. "Terrified," he admitted, exhaling sharply. "Terrified I'd ruin what we have before it even had a chance to grow."

Her fingers twitched, brushing briefly against the edge of the console, a small, almost imperceptible motion that was both a test and a signal. Jackson's eyes followed, and his chest tightened—not with panic this time, but with the raw pull of hope.

"And now?" she asked, her voice softening further, carrying a weight of both challenge and invitation.

Jackson's lips pressed into a thin line as he met her gaze fully. "Now… now I tell you everything. No more secrets," he said, voice firming with determination. "Because if we're going to do this… if we're going to be us… it has to be built on truth. Every bit of it. No lies. Not for me, not for you."

Jaida studied him, her body still taut with unspoken emotion, her mind racing but her heart slowly unclenching.

The tension between them didn't vanish, but it shifted—no longer a wall, but a fragile bridge. She nodded once, slowly, deliberately. "Okay," she said, the single word carrying both acceptance and challenge, a quiet permission for him to keep talking.

Jackson's hand moved, brushing lightly over hers, fingertips grazing in a silent reassurance. "I'm here," he murmured, low and certain. "I'm not going anywhere. Not now. Not ever."

The night stretched around them—still, quiet, intimate—and for the first time since the confession, it felt like they might just make it through. Together.

Jaida's chest felt tight, every inhale heavy, every exhale a slow surrender to the storm of disbelief and hurt coursing through her. The moonlight slanted through the windshield, casting streaks across the dashboard, flickering across Jackson's face. It highlighted the tension in his jaw, the faint crease between his brows, the vulnerability in his eyes. She could see it all, and it only made her heart ache.

She swallowed, voice barely above a whisper. "How long... have you known?"

Jackson's eyes flicked to hers, a shadow of pain crossing his features. He hesitated, as if measuring the weight of the truth in his own chest. "Not long," he admitted, voice rough. "Just... a few months."

Jaida blinked, the words like shards against her tongue. "A few of months," she repeated softly, almost to herself, her voice trembling with the weight of realization. "You've known for a couple of months... and you let me—" her hands twisted in her lap, "—fall in love with you without knowing the full truth?"

Jackson swallowed, the movement tight in his throat. His hands hovered, then retreated to the wheel, as if fearing that any touch would shatter her further. "It was before we met. I—I didn't know how to do it right," he said, voice low, rough. "Every time I thought I'd tell you, something... I don't know, stopped me. I couldn't risk you walking away. I can't lose you."

The blunt had burned down to ash in the console, the smoke lingering like a memory between them. Jaida's eyes flicked to it, then back to him. She could see the fear and regret twisting in his features, see the desperate longing that mirrored her own conflicting emotions—anger, hurt, and the undeniable pull toward him.

"And now?" she asked, voice steadier than she felt. "Now that I know?"

Jackson exhaled sharply, shoulders slumping slightly as he turned fully toward her. The shadows of the car wrapped them in a cocoon, safe and private. "Now…" His hand finally reached across the space between them, hovering just above hers. "Now I tell you everything. No more holding back. No more half-truths. I'm done being afraid. I want to be honest with you, fully. You deserve that."

Jaida's pulse raced, and for a moment, all she could hear was the rhythm of her own heart. The quiet of the street outside seemed suspended, every distant car, every rustling leaf, muted by the tension in the car. She could feel the weight of his gaze on her, a mixture of fear, hope, and the raw need for her to understand, to stay.

"You're scared," she said, almost whispering, her eyes searching his. "But so am I. You've given me a thousand reasons to trust you… but you've also just given me a reason to question everything."

Jackson nodded slowly, his thumb brushing lightly against the back of his hand in nervous anticipation. "I know," he admitted. "I know I've put that on you. But I promise… I'll make it right. I'll show you every day. I'll earn your trust, even if it takes everything I have."

The tension in the car shifted subtly, like a tide pulling back before a wave. Jaida's lips parted, her defenses trembling under the pull of everything they'd shared, everything she still felt. She wanted to recoil, to push him away, but the warmth of him, the honesty in his eyes, anchored her in the moment.

Finally, she exhaled, a slow, trembling breath, and let her hand inch toward his. Their fingers met halfway, brushing, lingering, connecting in a silent truce.

Jackson's chest rose and fell with relief he hadn't realized he'd been holding back. His thumb stroked the back of her hand lightly, reverently, as if she were a fragile flame he feared to snuff out.

Jaida's fingers traced faint circles on the fogged-up window, each motion trembling slightly, betraying the calm mask she wore. The street outside was quiet, shadows stretching long beneath the flicker of a lone streetlight. The air in the car smelled faintly of smoke and her perfume, the lingering scent of their earlier closeness, warm and sharp against the cool night.

"But what about me?" Jaida asked, turning her head slightly so her profile caught the light from the streetlamp. "You weren't afraid of how it would feel for me to find out... like this?"

He closed his eyes, a sharp exhale slipping past his lips as if the words themselves were knives. "I was afraid of losing you," he whispered, voice low, trembling. "But now… now, I might lose you anyway."

The sound of crickets outside, punctuated by a distant car passing, wrapped around them. The headlights swept across her face for a fleeting moment, illuminating the faint sheen of tears she refused to release. Every shadow in the car seemed to hold its own kind of tension—thick, unspoken, almost tangible.

Jaida leaned back, her head pressing lightly against the headrest, staring at the roof as if the ceiling could answer her questions. Her chest ached with a heaviness that made every inhale deliberate. Her lips parted once, then pressed together again as she forced herself to hold the storm inside.

"You made me feel safe," she finally whispered, voice catching in her throat. "I let my guard down with you. That's not something I do easily."

Jackson's hand hovered, inches from hers, trembling slightly. "I know," he said softly. "I know, and I'm so sorry." His eyes, dark and raw, bore into hers, begging for understanding that he didn't know if he deserved.

For a long moment, they simply existed in the car together, the silence heavy but full—full of regret, of love, of fear, of longing. The air between them seemed to pulse, almost breathing, echoing the storm that had just landed in the quiet of the night.

Finally, Jaida exhaled, shaky and uncertain. "I need time," she said, barely above a whisper.

Jackson parted his lips, searching for words, then closed them again, his thumb brushing over his own hand in a small gesture of restraint. He nodded slowly, deliberately. "I'll wait," he said, voice low, steady despite the ache in his chest. "As long as you need."

She didn't answer—not at first. Her heart was still sprinting ahead of her, caught between the longing to forgive and the dread of being shattered again. Silence held her for a moment before her lips finally parted, her words drifting out more to herself than to him.

"This... this wasn't in the forecast," she said, eyes drifting back to the window where the unanticipated storm pressed against the glass in trembling sheets, mirroring the chaos in her mind. "When things seem too good to be true, they usually are. I didn't see it coming. And now that it's here... I don't know if I'm supposed to run from it or stand in the rain and let it wash everything away."

Jackson shifted closer, the dim glow of the streetlight catching the damp shine gathering at the corners of his eyes. "Then let me stand with you," he said, his voice a quiet vow. He hesitated, studying her face before he continued in a voice barely above a whisper. "I know you've already weathered so many storms, Jaida. Maybe this one feels heavier than the rest—but storms don't last forever. And when this one passes... I believe there'll be a rainbow waiting on the other side. Not because everything will be perfect—but because we made it through together."

She didn't say yes. She didn't say no.

The car sat suspended on the edge of the driveway, two people caught between fear and hope, the storm outside echoing the one inside. Neither knew if the next moment would bring clearing skies—or the next, relentless wave. And in that pause, that fragile, aching silence, they existed together. Waiting. Feeling. Standing at the edge of everything they feared.

Jackson's chest tightened, every nerve on edge as he watched her. Fear and longing tangled in his gaze, and even though they were only inches apart, it felt as though an ocean had opened between them. "Jaida... please," he whispered, his voice rough, strained with a vulnerability he rarely allowed himself to show. "Say something. Anything. Don't... don't close this off."

She didn't turn to him. Instead, she leaned closer to the window, letting the cold glass press gently against her fingertips.

The moonlight dripped over her features, soft and teasing, illuminating the tension in her jaw and the subtle trembling of her shoulders.

Her eyes followed its slow, imperceptible drift across the sky, as though it carried the answer he needed. Her heart thudded painfully in her chest, a rhythm that screamed both longing and restraint. And yet, her voice, when it came, was calm and deliberate: "Goodnight, Jackson."

The words landed in the air between them like fragile glass. Jackson's gaze drank her in—the silhouette of her neck, the quiet grace in the way she held herself, the unspoken storm behind her eyes. Every detail seared itself into him: the softness of her voice, the weight of her silence, the impossible pull of her presence.

"Goodnight, Jaida," he whispered back, voice hoarse, almost breaking, as if speaking it aloud could tether them closer despite the space her words had carved. He memorized her there, in the pale glow of the moon, a mixture of strength and fragility he was helpless to resist, knowing this moment would haunt him long after the night swallowed its light.

Jaida stepped out of the car slowly. The door clicked shut behind her, sharp and resonant, as if the night itself had marked the moment.

Rain slicked the pavement, droplets catching the pale streetlights like scattered diamonds. The cold air hit her skin, sharp and insistent, brushing through her hair and chilling the nape of her neck. She didn't look back. The storm followed—thundering in the sky above, and worse, coiling inside her chest.

Her keys pressed into her palm, metal biting softly into her fingers, grounding her as she walked. Each step on the wet asphalt was deliberate, measured, as if she could step through the ache by sheer will. The wind tugged at her coat, whispering secrets she didn't want to hear.

Inside, silence met her like a living thing. No hum of the refrigerator, no muted TV, no background music—only the faint tick of the clock, heavy and steady.

She slipped off her damp shoes; the soft thud against the hardwood echoed in the emptiness. She moved to the kitchen, automatic, ritualistic—keys clattering onto the counter, cabinet doors creaking open, glass in hand. She reached for the Pinot Grigio reserved for nights like this: quiet, private, weighted with intention. The cork popped, a small exhalation, and the aroma filled the air: crisp pear, white peach, something like solace.

Outside, Jackson sat in the car, hooded by shadow. Rain traced slow, glimmering trails down the windshield. He gripped the wheel, knuckles tight, heart pounding in sync with the patter of the rain.

The car smelled faintly of smoke, leather, and her lingering presence. Every sound—the drip from the roof, the distant bark of a dog, the faint vibration of the city—was amplified, a symphony of memory and longing.

Jaida moved to the bathroom. The dim vanity light cast halos around her reflection, softening the edges she didn't want to examine. She turned the faucet; hot water roared into the tub, steam curling and twisting, wrapping the room in warmth.

A single candle flickered on the tub's edge, shadows dancing across the walls, the light trembling as if it too were holding its breath.

She undressed slowly, letting each piece fall like shedding the weight of the day. Stepping into the water, the heat embraced her skin, hot and insistent, yet incapable of reaching the cold ache coiled in her heart. Wine glass balanced in hand, she leaned back, letting the water cradle her while her eyes closed against the heaviness she carried.

No music. No thoughts she could pin down. Only the rhythm of her own breath: In. Out. In. Out. No tears. Not yet.

Outside, the world moved without care. Stars blinked overhead, cold and distant. Crickets sang their indifferent lullaby. A porch light flickered. Somewhere, a car door slammed. Somewhere else, a dog barked. The storm in the sky had slowed, leaving only drizzle and the occasional low rumble of distant thunder.

Inside the car, Jackson felt time stop, thick and viscous, yet impossibly heavy with expectation. Every detail lingered: the sway of her hair, the curve of her shoulder. Every heartbeat, every breath, every silent word left behind carved its mark.

Jackson exhaled, slow and deliberate, the sound lost in the drum of the rain. "This was the cost of honesty," he whispered to himself, voice low, heavy, carried into the quiet. His pulse matched the rhythm of the windshield's rain, steady and restless. He leaned back, closing his eyes, letting the darkness of the night and the memory of her presence press into him.

Jaida rested her head against the back of the tub, eyes closed. Steam curled around her, wrapping her in temporary protection. Her breath was steady, measured. She let the water soak her skin, let the heat hug her body, let the quiet wrap around her mind.

And still, outside, Jackson waited. For clarity. For forgiveness. For her.

The calm after *The Unanticipated Storm* wasn't peace. It was quiet uncertainty—dense, tangible, unrelenting. And it was real. He would sit in that stillness—for as long as it took.

The End.

The storm is just beginning! Danielle Amour is the up-and-coming author that you'll want to keep on your radar! If you enjoyed this novel, keep in touch by following the author on social media.

Instagram:
@danielleamourwrites
Booking Email:
danielleamourwrites@gmail.com

Stay Connected!

Danielle Amour

www.ingramcontent.com/pod-product-compliance
Lightning Source LLC
Chambersburg PA
CBHW030636110726
47901CB00002B/473